"A triumphant fir   ady known through he   fac- tually researched   ent for story-telling -   the night, unable to tear myself away . . . A gripping tale with suspense on every page."

(Lynn Montgomery, *Aberdeen Press & Journal*)

"From her immensely successful autobiographies Marianne MacKinnon turns to fiction in this drama that whirlwinds around Claire's comfortable city marriage and racy Florentine affaire. A sensual and stunning fresco of the true colour of love. *The Deluge* is a dream of a first novel. Fact or fantasy . . . you won't put the light out until you finish this Wellsian journey."

(John Ryan, *Glasgow Evening Times*)

"Marianne MacKinnon's first venture into fiction is as vivid and enthralling as her eminently readable autobiographies. Cleverly constructed and beautifully observed, *The Deluge* is a powerful novel with a strong sense of drama and characterization."

(David Burness, *Sunday Post*)

MARIANNE MACKINNON

Ms MacKinnon was born in Berlin in 1925. Her two highly acclaimed volumes of autobiography, *The Naked Years* and *The Alien Years*, tell the story of her life in Hitler's Germany and during the Second World War, then in postwar England and Berlin, and in the Italy and Spain of the early 1950s. Winner of several literary awards, Marianne MacKinnon has three sons and lives in Scotland. *The Deluge* is her first novel. Her present work in progress (1993) is a political thriller set in East Germany before and after The Wall.

Also by Marianne MacKinnon

The Naked Years

The Alien Years

The Deluge

a tale of Florence in flood

Marianne MacKinnon

HILLCREST BOOKS

First published in 1993 by
Hillcrest Books
Torrance, Glasgow G64 4HF, Scotland

© Marianne MacKinnon 1993

Typeset in Scotland by Black Ace Editorial
Ellemford, Duns, TD11 3SG

Cover designed in Scotland by Smith & Paul Associates
Acer Crescent, Paisley, PA2 9LN

Printed in Great Britain by Antony Rowe Ltd
Chippenham, Wiltshire, SN14 6QA

All rights reserved. Strictly except in conformity with the provisions of the Copyright Act 1956 (as amended), no part of this book may be reprinted or reproduced or exploited in any form or by any electronic, mechanical or other means, whether such means be known now or invented hereafter, including photocopying, or text capture by optical character recognition, or in any information storage or retrieval system, without permission in writing from the publisher. Any person or organization committing any unauthorized act in relation to this publication may be liable to criminal prosecution and civil action for damages. Marianne MacKinnon is identified as author of this work in accordance with Section 77 of the Copyright, Designs and Patents Act 1988.

A CIP catalogue record for this book
is available from the British Library

ISBN   0 9521447 0 0

Set in New Century Schoolbook
Using Telos Text Composition System TL4
Output through a Hewlett Packard LaserJet 4M

The author is grateful to the Scottish Arts Council for financial support which made possible essential factual research in Florence

The Deluge takes for part of its background the devastating flood which struck Florence on 4 November 1966, destroying or severely damaging many of the city's art treasures, causing great suffering to its population and claiming several lives. Although there exist faithful accounts of earlier floods (see *Appendix*), first recorded in 1333, when, following days of continuing rain, the river Arno burst its banks, none quite reached the cataclysmic scale of this modern deluge, notably because the authorities did not, or were unable, to issue a timely warning. Whereas historical events chronicled or associated with *L'Alluvione* are real and have taken place, the characters portrayed in this book, as well as their individual experiences, are invented, and no resemblance to any real person, living or dead, is intended or should be inferred.

*'And all the fountains of the great deep
were broken up . . . '*

*'And all the windows of heaven opened,
and the flood of waters was upon the earth . . . '*

'And the waters were abated from off the earth . . . '

'And the bow shall be in the cloud . . . '

(Genesis, 7/8)

E quelche mi convien ritrar testeso
non portò voce mai, né scrisse incostro
né fu per fantasia già mai compreso;

> *Dante Alligheri,*
> Paradiso, *XIX, 167*

Prologue

*And what I now must tell has never been
reported by a voice, inscribed by ink,
never conceived by the imagination;*

Dante, *Paradiso*, XIX, 167

No, I'm afraid I can't tell anyone. Quite simply because nobody would believe me. Some people would call my story an all too realistic dream; others, less delicately, a premenopausal fantasy. There are those who would bring Freud into the equation or quote from the case of a friend of a friend who suffered from a similar delusion and ended up *non compos mentis*. And, of course, I can't exclude the odd whisper weaving about behind my back, the arch intimation that my experiences are no more than wishful thinking.

Neither would my confession generate credulity in those dearest to me. Charles, for one, would initially opt for reticence. Having first ponderously busied himself with his pipe – a habit which always precedes serious deliberations or the structuring of an erudite reply to a critical question – I am sure he would look a me with the unshakability of a sage and the patience of what is whimsically referred to as a 'shrink'. And I know that he would wait for the telephone to ring or some urgent household task to claim my attention, if not for his pointed silence to spark off in me another subject of conversation, one less sensitive, less mystifying and lending itself to rational dialogue – anything to relieve him of a comment.

His reaction would speak for itself.

For not given to the study of natural phenomena, or personal experiences which are neither logically nor scientifically interpretable, he would jump at the chance to argue an abstract point, discuss a mundane problem or air his views on the university's financial policies, rather than examine the feasibility of my recent ordeal.

Paul, on the other hand, was likely to respond to my account with the ebullience and quick tongue of youth. He would slap his knee, call me a fine raconteur and, with a pinch of mockery in his voice, suggest a 'nice cup of tea' as the panacea for middle-aged flights of fancy. His recent excursion into the field of experimental psychology might even tempt him to mention Freud, and how the good doctor would have a field-day with dear Mum on his couch.

And there is Valerie, my dear friend and confidante. She would not blink if I told her I planned to take up missionary work in deepest Africa, or that, at the age of forty-four, I had got myself pregnant. Sleek, sophisticated and twice divorced, equally at home in her designer outfits as in baggy trousers and man-sized pullovers, she is known for her sharp wit and never mincing her words, even if this entails ruffling feathers or driving a point home with a sledgehammer.

Val, too, was bound to react predictably and in her own inimitable style. I have played out the scene many times in my head.

'My dear girl,' she replies to my strange and piquant divulgences, crossing her beautiful legs and slipping a cigarette into a dainty holder, 'look at yourself. You're an art historian and acknowledged authority on the Italian Renaissance. You've written two clever books, and your monthly magazine article is immensely readable, even for someone like myself, who admits to no more than a purely aesthetic appreciation of art. Besides, you're a good housewife and mother, not to speak of your skills as a hostess. Christ, I wish I were a wizard in the kitchen like you. Do you know, the Granger-Hamiltons are still raving about your last dinner-party? Really, Claire, what's got into you? Are you having me on?'

Now the scene grows burlesque.

'No, I'm not,' I counter Val's arguments, my voice a mere whisper, my normally imperturbable self clamouring for a single word or gesture which would suggest even a tentative acceptance of my account. But Val, at a loss for an emphatic response, and in order to buy time, lights her cigarette and blows ringlets of smoke into the air, before offering crude, practical advice.

'It's your hormones, of course. What you need, darling, is a double Martini, a new dress and – let me spell it out for you – a good screwing from Charles.' And warming up to the subject, she would talk of stress, mid-life appetites and the tricks a fertile mind can play on an unsuspecting body. That's the way she is, a good friend, well-meaning and outspoken. Inimical to all mysteries, she stands like a rock in the clear waters of realism.

No, I can't tell anyone.

But I shall write things down as they happened, a kind of intimate journal. It ought to get things out of my system. I shall write in longhand, for the passage of a pen over paper is silent, and each stroke will carry my personal imprint. It is also a more intimate medium than a typewriter. The pen's proximity to paper alone makes it a more honest, more courageous communicator. Meticulously, as it records, it will not shrink back from the abstruse or downright erotic. Ultimately, I intend to shred the pages and delegate them to the dustbin, thence to the city's incinerator. It will be a symbolic act, of course. Memories can't be made to go up in smoke. Only time can eradicate what does not fit into traditionally empiric patterns. I'm sure it will eventually blur, darken, pull to its depths whatever fragments of awe, doubt and wonder still persist in my mind.

1

Although I have been a contributor to the magazine for five years, Lewis will still heave his burly, balding self out of his editorial chair and offer me a generous handshake – a custom, I am told, he brought back from the States a few years ago, together with his Bostonian wife and a preference for Cuban cigars.

'Got any family commitments at the moment?' he inquired.

'No, nothing special,' I said. 'Charles is busy with the new term, and Paul has gone back to Cambridge.'

'What about work?'

'I'm doing a paper on Bella Robbia. My new evening class starts in a fortnight, and my next lecture at the Academy is not due until January.'

'Splendid! I've got an assignment for you. I'd like you to go to Florence next week.'

'Florence?' I echoed, smoothing a non-existing crease in my skirt.

'Yes, Florence. Remember the huge flood they had down there in sixty-six? On the fourth of November, to be precise.'

My emphatic nod was swept away by Lewis' enthusiasm for the potential this date held for the magazine.

'I hear the city is going to commemorate the twentieth anniversary of the disaster in style,' he said. 'I'd like to do a special on it. There'll be street exhibitions, public film and video shows. The lot. I'm sure the Italian press will give the event wide coverage, and Florence editions will dig up statistics and the memories of older residents. The flood damage was colossal at the time, as you will recall. I still remember one national headline: *The birthplace of the European Renaissance ravaged by water and mud.* I was a junior reporter at the time.'

'I remember,' I said. 'The international art world was shocked. My professor called it a desecration, and when he listed some of the victimised treasures, he had tears in his eyes. Anyway, what did you have in mind?'

'Well, Claire. You're familiar with the magazine. You know the ropes. Give me something on the restoration of the city's art treasures and books. Perhaps some background colour, local sentiments. I'll fix up an interview with the editor of the *Nazionale*, and John can come down from Milan to take some pictures. By the way, how's your Italian?'

'Still molte bene.'

'Great!' Under a beaming smile, Lewis loosened his flamboyant tie and swivelled to and fro in his chair as other men behind executive desks play with their pens or doodle.

'I say, you haven't been to Florence for some time, Claire, have you?'

'Not for twenty years. In fact, I missed the flood by less than two days.'

'And you never went back?'

'No!' My monosyllabic reply sounded flat and perhaps a trifle too resolute, for Lewis' eyes widened quizzically, forcing an explanation. I straightened my back and, with the eloquence of a defence lawyer, presented my arguments.

'Well,' I said, 'for one thing Charles and I got married shortly after I came back in sixty-six. Then I had Paul. Later, as I extended my studies of the Quattrocento, it was somehow always Rome or Venice, Ravenna or Perugia. And, during vacations, France. Charles is such a Francophile, you see. And we have that little old cottage in Provence, right out in the country. Complete with wooden beams, open hearth and mediaeval well. And you should see the garden. Old trees, shrubs, a profusion of flowers. Part of it is growing wild – a haven for bees and butterflies. And as for sounds, it's all a-humming and a-chirping, as they say. I call it my green spa. Charles, of course, likes to get literary. He says it's a place where he can spin green thoughts in a green shade.'

Lewis shook his head. 'It wouldn't do for me, I'm afraid. I need people and activity even on holiday. But fancy Charles taking to rural life so easily.'

'As if he were born to it.'

'Doesn't he get bored?'

'Never. He potters happily around all day in shorts and clogs. But then there's the added attraction of the local wine. It is excellent. It pulls down social barriers. By now, Charles doesn't only know half the village by their Christian names, but is also on 'thou' terms with the mayor. So you see . . . '

I took a deep breath and shared Lewis' amused smile. He was about to turn his attention to some papers on his desk, when the telephone rang and an editorial matter claimed his full concentration.

My mind instantly computed the possibilities ahead. Here, I thought, was my chance to go back. The time had come, and not too soon. I would walk tall and proud in the footsteps of my younger self – unafraid, single-minded, a woman rooted solidly in her marriage. I wouldn't think twice about squashing, like flies, the lustful little demons which had lately troubled my life, the rogues of fancy which kept creeping into bed with me at night, as if by right. A quick kill was surely the answer, then a clean burial, and may they rest forever . . .

Outside, a rare spectacle in London's concrete jungle, dry leaves sucked up by a gust of wind were whirling past the window. Lewis, still on the phone, articulated his doubts to the caller that a certain person would agree to an interview.

I was growing inches taller in my chair. I was in no doubt about my personal assignment in Florence.

2

Over Pisa airport the clouds were hanging so low that they seemed to touch the runway. My flight from London had been a comfortable one. I had not only enjoyed a complimentary bottle of Chianti, but also a mental detachment that enabled me squarely to face my task ahead.

As I stepped on to the tarmac, spongy humidity smothered my face and settled in my hair. I knew the locals would see no more than a seasonal occurrence in mist shrouding the Tuscan plains. For me, however, on this grey and melancholic afternoon, the reduced visibility and the onslaught of air drenched with billions of water particles, formed an uneasy setting to my personal resolution. I pulled up my coat collar, tightened the grip on my travel bag and quickened my pace. Amid the roar of departing aircraft I was conscious of my metal-tipped heels smacking the concrete in an ungiving staccato movement which underscored a sense of foreboding.

From my window seat I watched passengers boarding the coach for the transfer to Florence. An elderly lady, dressed in unrelieved grey, and stepping, spectre-like, out of the thickening mist, was last to mount the steps of the vehicle, and she did so with an agility that belied her years. Without touching my sleeve, without causing the air between us to ruffle, she sat down beside me.

I glanced at my neighbour, ready to play my guessing game which, whenever I was travelling in the company of strangers, and my mind enjoyed a curious lucidity, warded off boredom and intrigued me with its infinite variables.

The lady's eyes met mine, fleetingly, uncommittedly, the hint of a smile flashing across her face like distant lighting, yet long enough for me to photograph it in my mind: a gentle face with a touch of the ascetic. Steel-grey hair pulled back into a sober bun the size of a tennis ball and toning in with her outfit, except for a white streak running along her temple. An unobtrusive nose set over thin, bloodless lips. A face bare of life's harsh lines, yet equally of the crowfeet of easy laughter – the kind one often comes across in nuns, or in women used to disciplining or to masking their emotions.

Spinster-type, ex-school-mistress, country-lover, I categorized her. Someone who uses lavender soap and Nivea cream, and who loves the smell of sun-dried laundry. A gentle soul who feeds the birds in winter, keeps a cat, reads the Bible and is at home in the world of nineteenth century novelists.

I turned to the Lady in Grey, ready to probe my theory by way of casual conversation.

But she had closed her eyes.

However, the flicker of a muscle around the corner of her mouth, as well as her fidgety lips, revealed that she remained fully attentive to the murmur of conversation spilling into the aisle, and to any variation in the speed of the coach, while every now and again her hands fastened their grip on the huge horn handles of her petit-point bag. I mentally shrugged my shoulders and left my non-communicative neighbour to doze or abandon herself to her very private ruminations.

I did not realise at the time that my catching sight of her one day would be as welcome a landmark to me as the turrets and cupolae of the Holy City must have been to pilgrims in earlier centuries. Or that her sudden appearance on another occasion would baffle me until I had decoded her smile.

On the autostrada visibility was decreasing with every mile.

'*Nebbio maledetto!*' Cursing the fog, the driver reduced his speed.

I peered out of the window at a grey expanse in which roadside trees flashed past like ghosts. Soon the soporific hum of the coach's engine turned my eye inwards.

My plan was mapped out. My professional errands would leave me sufficient time for my private mission. I knew where to look for Paolo. A fine silver- and goldsmith, such as he had been twenty years ago, would surely have carried on his grandfather's business on the Ponte Vecchio – the prestigious locality for the city's jewellers and precious-metal artists.

I saw myself walking into his shop, looking leisurely at the display of delicate workmanship, perhaps expressing an interest in a particular item, while waiting for the moment when we would be out of earshot of customers and employees.

'Hello, Paolo. Remember me?' I'd say, devouring his dawning recognition, his surprise or embarrassment. His eyes might rest appreciatively on my smart Jaeger suit, my Hermes-style handbag, my Bally shoes; with male adroitness they might trace my figure which, though rounder and softer, I had kept trim by swimming my weekly self-prescribed twenty lengths, and by joining the neighbourhood's early-jogging brigade at a time when Charles was still sipping his morning tea or grunting in the shower.

Perhaps over a coffee or an *apéritivo* I would shoot the one question at Paolo, which for years has haunted me like the missing cord from a catching tune:

'And why did you return my letters marked "Addressee unknown"?'

Even now, as I chronicle my sweet obsession, I recall the tone of the letters I had written to him shortly after my return to London in sixty-six – desperate missives aching with longing and regrets, a testimony of my inner tug-of-war.

My decision to leave Florence at the end of six months of post-graduate research had been a realistic one, born out of common sense, the prudent sentinel which had always kept my emotive and adventurous spirit from making unwise decisions.

An early November mist had been hugging Florence, draining colours and adding visual emphasis to my resolution, when Paolo had caught me, studying a train timetable.

'Marry me, Claire,' he said. No more. He did not touch me, but I felt his eyes, his hands, his lips caressing and willing me to stay on.

But on this grey morning, with all my inner arguments settled, my emotions were not pliable.

'I can't, darling,' I pleaded. 'I want to write my thesis, and there's a part-time job waiting for me at a London gallery.' I did not look at Paolo, as I spoke of the career that beckoned, of the options that would crown years of hard study.

Excuses, explanations. How banal, how irrelevant they sounded. But how could I disclose my equally weighty reservations? My fear that – conservative as Paolo was in his ways, a child of family customs and local conventions – he might want to see me growing plump, soft and suppliant at his hearth, the mother of a proud line of bambini. And where was my guarantee that once I wore his wedding ring he would not shift towards the comfortable centuries-old chauvinistic attitudes of southern males? My sentiments about the Roman Catholic Church formed no less of an obstacle: the way I felt about her patriarchal omnipresence, however magnificent her places of worship; or my aversion, deep down, to confessionals, chants, swinging incense, liturgical cadences and rosaries – the manifestations of a faith that would find no resonance in me, who had grown up in less ritualistically rigid spiritual climes.

'I can't,' I repeated, my face pressed against the V of bronzed skin exposed by Paolo's open-neck shirt. Although summer was long gone, he seemed still to smell of sun, sand and the Thyrrenean Sea. For one wild moment I was ready to trade in all my career aspirations for a permanent place at his side, ready even to convert to Islam or join the Mormon Church, so why not fashion my life to the alien confines of Catholicism?

But then a cold shower of reasoning chilled my heart's waverings and allowed sobriety to settle the issue. My voice, however, could not hide the sadness within me, nor my own tender gestures the love I was sacrificing to my career ambitions.

'Then write to me, chiara,' said Paolo. 'Perhaps you'll change your mind and come back. And, sensing my reluctance to free myself from his arms, 'I know, you will.'

The last morning.
Rooms filled with the dreary light of a morose sky, casting washed-out shadows. As Paolo leaves, to meet an important American client in his grandfather's shop, we face each other. Everything has been said and words now weigh lightly, even smiles.

'See you for lunch, Claire. I'll take you to the station in the afternoon.'

My blood seems to drain away. I have to restrain myself from seeking a last fusion of arms and lips. For Paolo does not know that I shall be leaving for an earlier train.

'Ciao,' I breathe at him, breaking into a brave last-curtain smile and seeing him out.

Somewhere in the house a door slams, the sound of high-pitched voices surges into the stairways, deadening what is left of Paolo's presence. I am dying a little – my first experience of *partir c'est toujours mourir un peu*.

But this is how I want it: a brief farewell, like an execution. Not for me that slow exit at a station – compartment doors banging shut, tearing apart the last frantic touch, the last unspoken words. Waiting an eternity for the train to jerk forward and gain speed. The compulsive look out of the window, to see a face growing smaller, fading away . . .

By the time I was ready to leave that morning, the sky had turned murky and it was drizzling. I left a farewell note on the kitchen table, stroked Sarah and watered the hyacinth. Then I shouldered my pack and locked the door. I knew I was leaving behind more than memories, more than a broken comb, a piece of scented soap, a library copy of Petrarca's verse and a snapshot of myself in a bikini on Viareggio beach.

As I descended the stairs and stepped into the greyness of the street, I moved like a somnambulist. That is why I forgot about the house-key. Not until halfway between Florence and Milan did I find it in the inner zip-pocket of my anorak.

I cursed my forgetfulness.

After all, nice lodgers or long-term house-guests leave their host's door-key behind when they move on. I realise, of course, that force of habit had prevailed during the emotional turmoil of my departure. For ever since cooler weather had set in and I was wearing my anorak when out and about, I had deposited the key in this special pouch for safekeeping.

Today, surveying events from a safe, if uncertain, distance, and although tending to ignore earlier speculations, I find questions still fitfully arise in my mind, which will not yield to a rational explanation. Thus I am wondering – by way of mere hypothesis, of course – whether things might have taken a different turn, if I had pushed the key through the letter-box.

Or simply, if twenty years later, during my recent visit to the city, a whim of mine had not taken me first to the Choistro Verde that fateful morning, or my imaginary powers led me astray.

Back in London in sixty-six, I recall my friends commenting on the new softness of my features and, two weeks later, inquiring solicitously about the dark crescents under my eyes. What they did not know was that my letters to Paolo had come back, unopened, blue envelopes defaced by official stamps and some illegible scribble. I recall days of aching and walking as if blindfolded, nights spent tossing and turning in the sterility of my bed. I felt raw and confused and angry, all in one. And, again, only common sense prevented me from rushing back to Florence and making my life with Paolo.

I had been so young, so vulnerable, so hellishly sensible.

It was not long, however, before I realised that the restoration of my equilibrium was priority number one. Stop the lamentations, I told myself. Eat the food you chose, sleep in the bed you made for yourself.

I applied myself assiduously to my work, and for spare-time activities devised a formula for some light-hearted promiscuity – the popular game which demands no commitment of the players and stops short of the heart.

A novice in fleeting relationships, I threw myself into the dating ring. I went out with a right-wing political columnist of a provincial paper, who wore his intentions on his sleeve and knew every pub in town; I made it to the untidy sitting-room of a sociologist who talked Marx over a Chinese take-away and a glass of acidic wine, before inviting me to admire his etchings; I had myself champagned and dined into a hopefully seducible mood by a handsome airline pilot from Iowa, who – at the mercy of flight rosters – had long abandoned lengthy conversational overtures in favour of gift-wrapped, snappily-packaged one-night affairs.

I slept with none of them, thereby spurning the rules of the game and, in turn, being dropped from it as a spoilsport. Like a virus resistant to casual relationships, my memory of Paolo had grown into a lingering malady which stopped me from flinging myself, fancy-free, into a round of insouciant or frivolous pleasures. It also forestalled any desire in me to fall in love again.

That is, until I met Charles.

Charles had the right medicine for my affliction. Ten years my senior, he courted me with flowers, subdued gestures and an inexhaustible arsenal of patience. He was kind and thoughtful, standing in my emotional steppe like the Eiffel Tower. Acting father, friend and treasured companion, he was also a man who did not resent his poor bargain, for all I had to offer at the time was my sore, sad self.

As the days grew shorter, and the first Christmas lights went up in Oxford Street, I fell in love with Charles. Not to the sound of blaring trumpets, but to the mellifluous strains of Mendelssohn's Violin Concerto.

A graduate of Cambridge and the Sorbonne, Charles was a lecturer in French Studies. When I met him he was in the running for a senior lectureship. His publications spoke for themselves: a paper on Proust, a monograph on some underrated French eighteenth-century poet, which had aroused more than polite interest in academic quarters, and more recently a textbook on the French Éclaircissement, highly acclaimed by the educational media for its originality of thought. Academically voracious, a single-minded scholar, he was bound to go far in his career.

He was also easy to look at. Tall and lean, his greenish eyes reflected clarity of thought and a gentle disposition, while his brown hair, which was beginning to edge away at the temples, kept shy of the high forehead. He looked distinguished even in an open-neck shirt.

One day his time came.

I was tearing up my letters to Paolo, in a slow, ritual act, glancing but cursorily at the outpourings of the writer, in which the heart and mind were engaged in trench-warfare. Totally absorbed in what I was doing, I did not hear the door bell. Suddenly Charles stood in the room, watching my stony face and my severance with the past. He asked no questions, but I knew he understood the symbolism of my action.

'The door was half open, Claire,' he said. 'And I did ring.'

I tossed the last fragment of a letter into the wastepaper basket.

'It's all right, Charles. I took the rubbish down earlier. I must have forgotten . . . ' My voice trailed off. I was turning over another page in the book of my life.

Charles took me into his arms as gingerly as the moment commanded. As we stood in silent communion with each other, the seconds booming away, the frigid calm inside me shattered. My senses recorded the fresh scent of soap and aftershave, the softness of cashmere wool, the nestling quality of arms, the firmness of muscles and sinews.

My body was reawakening to its sensuality.

And now flutes and clarinets played a lyrical tune which the leading violin picked up and spun into a poem of infinite sweetness. Something behind my sternum ached with the dulcet sound, and I rejoiced in the sudden knowledge that I was falling in love again.

'Marry me, darling,' said Charles, softly, as if he were treading on sacred ground. And steadying his voice, 'You may feel that this is not the right moment for a proposal, and I, too, would have preferred a more suitable setting for it, but something tells me that right now is the time to tell you that I love you, and that I'd like you to become my wife. Will you think about it?'

The violin rose to a majestic finale in sonata form, and I was still listening to the euphony within me by the time the applause broke and the musicians took their bow. I smiled at Charles, the soloist.

'I don't have to think about it.'

Charles had rushed me into marriage.

'The Christmas holidays are coming up, darling. Fancy a honeymoon in the Austrian Alps? A white Christmas, sledge-rides, skiing on powdered snow? Also, there's the house. When my parents died, I thought of selling it and moving into a smaller one. But it's such a fine old place. I'm sure you'd like it. We could have it redecorated while we're away. You might want new furniture, a new bedroom suite . . . And what about furnishing your own study? You could write your thesis there and later apply for a lectureship.'

How all of a sudden the frontiers of my life had opened up wide. How they revealed vistas which reminded the music lover in me of the final movement of Beethoven's Pastoral Symphony, after-the-storm music so memorably transposed to technicolour in Disney's 'Fantasia' – a sky freed from the storm's anger, and ridding itself of the last straggling clouds. Trees, cornfields, pastures, rain-sated, their colours enhanced. Water droplets glistening in the sunshine, brooks bubbling lustily through meadows – a landscape dotted with cornflowers and poppies, over which a rainbow arched symbolically.

A small wedding, followed by weeks of snow, mulled wine, cheese fondue and strudels. Of skis making their tracks through virgin snow, and riding in a horse-drawn sledge to the ding-a-ling of little bells. Of dancing to a smoochy après-ski band or to rustic polka rhythms.

Happiness.

The kind that is not too greedy, nor apprehensive of its brittleness, and which seeks in the intimacies of the flesh but one of its permutations.

Ten years later, with two more books to his credit, Charles was offered a chair in French Studies. By then he had grown into a pillar of the Arts Faculty, being highly regarded for his quiet, scholarly ways, and for his vision, which tolerated no tunnel approach.

As husband and wife we never quarrelled in the nasty sense of the word. We never do. Simply because we still seldom find any difference of opinion worth quarrelling over. And not only are we mature, indeed fortunate, enough to subscribe to the premise that to allow the sun to set over a marital rift is to cleave something irreparable between partners, but both of us also abhor verbal warfare. We know that words spoken in acrimony or untempered anger have a habit of leavening, and of lingering in rooms, tactile and tenebrous. That it is important to remain flexible in our attitudes and modus operandi. Thus it has always come naturally to us to discuss any problem, and any disparity in our approach to it, as dispassionately and analytically as we would deal with a contentious issue in the lecture room. Besides, Charles' ability to acknowledge my younger and more volatile horizons tends to be a great leveller.

The birth of our son sent Charles into a parental orbit.

'What shall we call him?' he asked.

My eyes lost themselves in the whiteness of the hospital duvet. My voice was thin.

'Paul?'

Charles hesitated fractionally, then he patted my hand and smiled:

'Why not, darling, it's a good name. Come, let me hold the baby. I have a lot to learn. Fatherhood is such a serious business.'

Now greying and bespectacled, his shoulders hunching under the weight of centuries of French thought, if not under the department's financial problems, he is still cutting a fine figure behind the lectern, on panels and social platforms. Once asked by an interviewer which factors dominated his private life, he replied, 'My wife and my son are my co-ordinates', before doggedly leading the questioner into less intimate territory.

At home his study is his sanctum, our living-room his family resort, our bedroom his cathedral of privacy. He plays a fine game of golf, and I suspect that apart from the golfer's infatuation with the little white ball and the challenge of fairways, pars and birdies, he uses the green solitude of the course as the playing field for his alter ego.

Charles loathes official parties, especially those of the departmental kind, where familiar faces crowd in too cramped a space; where colleagues, secretaries and technicians stand around, sipping wine too sweet or too sour, while balancing paper plates loaded with paté, cheese, cold sausage rolls or Black Forest gâteau. Where talk between the men never ventures beyond university walls, and females communicate on domestic wavelengths.

Always the centre of attraction on such occasions,

sought out by post-graduates and junior lecturers for the privilege of a private word in his ear, or by senior colleagues for an off-the-record dissection of future university policies, Charles always stands out – like a Doric column – among the alcohol-flushed faces, daring ties and lowered necklines.

Paul adores his father.

As a toddler he used to sneak into his study while he was working. Respecting his father's keen concentration and the monastic silence of the room, content to remain within the radius of a paternal smile, he would sit on the carpet for hours, leafing through an old illustrated Bible or pretending to read whichever clever book might come within his reach.

In the nursery, Charles often lowered his lofty self to the floor, to help the youngster build a brick tower, or to put a derailed toy train back on its tracks. He read to him Aesop's Fables, stories from the Arabian Nights and the mythical Land of Cockaigne; he told him about Noah's Ark, Ulysses, Gargantua, King Arthur and the Three Wonders of Babylon. Above all, he instilled in him a love of books and classical values. He taught him how to ride his first bike.

And, no less appreciated by the teenager, he gave him driving lessons, showed him how to swing a golf club and tested him orally on French irregular verbs.

While Charles opened up to Paul worlds in which he was himself at home, I introduced my son to music and the arts – to my concept of beauty, and the things that are said to be hovering between heaven and earth. I will not forget the first time I took Paul out into the garden one night, to look at the clear, starlit August sky, while I tried to explain, in a toddler's language, my own orthodox faith in an Almighty, somewhere beyond man's limited perception of Space. And with my work centering on the Italian Renaissance, it did not come as a surprise to Charles and myself that over the years Paul developed an interest in everything Italian.

Now, at the age of nineteen, a second-year student in Italian Studies, Paul prides himself in showing his father how to change a tap-washer or strip the carburettor. Nothing, however, puts greater spring into his trainers than beating him at golf. I smile at the memory of Paul patting his progenitor on the back after winning by two strokes one weekend, saying, 'Never mind, Dad, only two down. Well played!'

When had things started to go wrong for me? Well, I needn't rack my brains, for the incident which had triggered off my emotional Odyssey is pretty much burnt into my mind. Perhaps if I had laughed aloud at myself, perhaps if I had taken up the study of Arabic or spring-cleaned the house until my bones ached, I might have been able to stop its perverse wanderings. Even a cold shower at bedtime could have done the trick. But then, my madness came overnight, and the corruption of my senses was instantaneous, as though an ill seed had fallen on fallow ground . . .

The scent of wet soil and chrysanthemums had been drifting into the house through the open patio doors, when Paul returned from his summer trip through Tuscany. Making a grand entrance from the terrace, he stood in the door, a six-foot-plus copy of Michelangelo's David in washed-out jeans, T-shirt and lumber jacket. He opened his arms the width of a primaeval bird.

'I'm back,' he cried, and with perfect intonation, *'Come stà, ma bella mamma?'* A peck on my cheek having completed the greeting, he divested himself of his jacket.

I could not take my eyes off him. How handsome he looked, how three months abroad had turned him into a man. Just then, an echo seemingly resounding from the other side of the world, snuggled itself back into my mind:

'*Ma bella Clairissima.*'

Suddenly my lips took on a life of their own. 'Paolo,' they breathed, and for a fleeting moment I saw my son through the eyes of my love-struck younger self, while my maternal instincts instantly, yet all too feebly, protested against such an improper exchange of images.

Paul took me by my shoulders.

'You look pale, Mum. Everything all right?'

'I'm fine, I said. 'How long can you stay, darling?'

'A few days. Term starts on Monday. How's Dad?' And not waiting for my answer, 'I say, I'm absolutely starving!'

'Why don't you have a quick shower and change?' I suggested. 'In the meantime I'll cook you some breakfast.'

'Bacon, eggs, tomatoes, toast, orange juice and strong coffee?'

'Yes, the lot.' I smiled, picked up the jacket from the satin-covered chair and closed the patio doors. To all appearances life was back on its old familiar tracks.

But it was not.

That night my bed turned into a pit of seduction.

As was his custom, Charles was reading in bed, something philosophical or abstract which, he claimed, lulled his brain into sleep. A quick good-night kiss. 'Sleep well, darling. I'll read for a few minutes.'

'Good night, Charles.'

Normally I would turn over, away from the light, and soon fall asleep. But not that night.

My mind and body were in disarray.

How rigid, how dispassionate our bedtime ritual had grown over the years, I thought. Not that love was absent. On the contrary, Charles and I adored each other. More as if love had tired of being demonstrative or innovative, tired of proving itself climactically, when words and gestures could express it so much more beautifully and nobly. In twenty years of marriage, our love-making had never set off grand fireworks, never totally lost itself in its consummation. As if it feared that carnal abandon might be inimical to the kinship of our minds or the purity of our love. By such definition it is perhaps not surprising that sexual forays had finally, and all too prematurely, become a Saturday-night fixture. Like a visit to the hairdresser or supermarket, a regular diary entry, a most agreeable weekend ceremony enacted with gentle decorum, never regretted, never anticipated with more than a flutter of the senses.

But tonight I kept tossing and turning.

'Is the light bothering you, darling?' asked Charles, carefully adjusting the beam of his bedside lamp away from my side of the duvet.

And now, plunged into a velvety semi-darkness, the images of Paul and Paolo fused. Magnificent maleness slipped into my bed and lifted my nightdress. It touched my breasts and lips, and I did not protest when a strong hand slid up my thigh. But now, and not a second too early, Paolo claimed the field as his own. I was back on Viareggio beach, back in the soft, shuttered bedroom light of his flat in Florence. I suppressed a sigh, and when I was unable to bear the exquisite torture any longer, I put out a hand towards Charles and groped for the familiar purlieus of warm, furry skin, for the limpness which rose and stiffened under my touch.

I had turned into a mendicant.

Charles looked at me over the rim of his glasses, his eyebrows arched in surprise at my overt solicitation. Slowly, as was his habit, he took off his glasses and returned them to their case with a click. He inserted his Moroccan leather bookmark into his book and closed it as ponderously as if he had come to the end of a satisfying read. He then wound up his bedside clock and switched off the light – as he always did, as he would do tomorrow and the night thereafter. And he – in the image of the young, handsome Paolo – made love to me.

That incident set a pattern. While during the day my sober, moral self denounced the nocturnal revelry of its subconscious, it was unable to control my bedtime fantasies. I blamed a freak mid-forties hormonal thrust, and a life lived too long, too greedily, among the Olympians of the Italian Renaissance, during which I had shared their passions painted on canvas, cut into stone or pursued in the bedchambers of palazzi.

As the days passed I experienced a sense of guilt and, in the cold light of another morning, disgust for my erotic drifting. But my self-reproaches did not restore me to the cosy comforts of conjugal life, and Paolo's handsome ghost continued to haunt my nights . . .

The coach's soporific hum failed to put my mind into lower gear. Weary of its fitful retrospectives, it began to argue and conjecture and visually to distort the image it had recently so alluringly, so potently reproduced.

I shall have to keep a cool head, I told myself, in order to avoid indulging even in the briefest of playful evocations of those happy months, whether for the sake of nostalgia or emotional self-flagellation. No more boiled sweets of reminiscences for me, but the erasure of an image.

It should be easy.

For Time is no custodian of beauty, and Paolo was no Dorian Gray. Twenty years could surely play havoc with a man's looks. They could leave him with a paunch and a receding hairline, etch every sin on his face or turn him into a hedonist, a selfish brute or a solid citizen with gold-capped teeth, toupé and horn-rimmed glasses. Or into a papier-mâché figure bogged down by cirrhosis of the liver, piles and a robot-like existence. And twenty years could easily affect a man's soul with middle-aged rot.

Another image beckoned:

Paolo successful like his grandfather, dressing as sedately as befitted his trade, and putting gloss on his business smile every morning as routinely as his assistant on the shop's most precious exhibits. Perhaps he owned a villa in Fiesole or San Domenico; perhaps he had married a Fiorentina who shopped in the Via Tornabuoni and left her husband enough freedom occasionally to play around with a pretty strumpet from the Piazza della Republica, whenever sexual boredom or the familiarity of the marital bed was itching his crotch.

But what, I asked myself, if through adverse circumstances he had ended up in one of the artisans' shops in the Oltrano or Frederiano quarter, doomed to make cheap jewellery for working girls and housewives?

A picture took shape in my mind: Paolo sitting in his tenement kitchen, stringing garlic bulbs or reading *L'Unità*. Paolo, among the noisy comings and goings of numerous children, heckling back at his vociferous wife whose figure, uncorseted, bloated by bambini, pasta and a predilection for tortiglioni, no longer matched conventional dress sizes.

And his love-making.

I knew I must not draw the line when it came to pronouncing the death sentence on the virile body that had lately invaded my waking dreams. Obediently my mind sketched a man of lacquered charm, a womaniser, a middle-aged Don Giovanni of the Casine or Florentine salons, one who had traded in the one-time poetry of his love for promiscuity, and who had pawned that tenderness – with which he had once serenaded his way in and out of my arms – for frenzied sex.

A glutton for the abuse of my mental effigy, I tried to envisage his love-making as it might have cheapened over the years: a roughened routine seeking no more than a pair of thighs, aiming at no more than the object of gratification. Hands that raised skirts like a tornado, a body which locked its victims to a mattress or the back of his car for as long as it took his spasms to ebb away . . .

I shifted uncomfortably in my seat. How vivid one's imagination can grow, how elephantine, when one is set to soil a memory which one would rather keep safely behind glass.

I stole a glance at my neighbour, who was studying a map of Florence and making entries into a notebook. In a speculative flash I saw the mousy lady saving up for her trip, perhaps to mark her retirement or grant herself a long-nourished wish. She would have done her homework on the city long before her departure, borrowing books from the library, her head spinning with the prospect of shortly coming face to face with the works of some of the greatest masters of the Renaissance. Once in Florence, she would tick off each night the paintings and sculptures and friezes and architectural grand slams she had viewed during the day, feeling privileged and richer for each experience, and planning the next day's programme while massaging her tired feet.

Notwithstanding the differences in our age and appearance, as well as the gap between my own scholarly knowledge and the lady's tourist-geared interests, I concluded that we were both pursuing a quest: my neighbour for the sight of some of the pinnacles of western culture, I for the exorcising of a ghost.

Outside, the mist was thinning, and out of the haze there now rose the contours of trees and the first outposts of urban spread. Then the city dressed in sombre light bore down on us. The river Arno, steel-grey and limpid. Fine buildings sighing under the the weight of age, air pollution and seasonal fatigue. Avenues pounding with traffic, glistening in the drizzle. Florence in monochrome.

It was the first of November, 1986.

3

The hotel, a former Medici palazzo, stood in a narrow street close to the Piazza Maria de Novella, its noble, if dilapidated façade hiding a modern-style interior vaguely described nowadays as 'international'. Apart from its vaulted and stuccoed ceiling, the large lobby could have been anywhere in the world – where glass, steel, plastic, huge ashtrays and twentieth-century prints and posters welcome the visitor with cool detachment. My eye, however, was quick to detect at least one witness to former patrician splendour: a Florentine mirror in an octagonal gilt frame, which hung forlornly, a proud alien, between an abstract painting and a 'Sunset over the Arno' watercolour.

The receptionist, a lady of fierce Italian looks and generous mid-life proportions, affected the self-assurance and authority of the proprietress. She handed me the room key with an inquisitive smile which manacled me to her desk. A momentary lull in guest traffic prompted the question:

'Perhaps the signora is interested in some of the events which commemorate the *Alluvione* in sixty-six?' She reached for a leaflet.

I said I was, briefly outlining the reason for my professional assignment. This fuelled communication, and soon the lady voiced her delight at my speaking fluent, if slightly rusty, Italian. I looked at the white-washed walls.

'How far did the water rise in here?' I wondered.

A fleshy finger pointed to a spot not far from the ceiling.

'Right up there. My family and the guests were marooned upstairs for two days. You won't see the water mark any more. It took years of redecorating, before it vanished. You see, the local stone is so porous.'

Professional interest must have shown on my face, for the signora's loquaciousness now flowed like a river in spate. Her husband, she divulged, had bought the building, a private residencia, shortly after the war, lock stock and barrel, together with many beautiful pictures, rugs and items of fifteenth- and sixteenth-century furniture among it.

'You should have seen this hall at the time of the flood,' she said. 'Chairs and tables were swimming on the water. So were paintings washed out of their frames. And the smell! Later, when the water had gone down, things stuck in the mud, either warped, broken or befouled with naphtha. The oil was everywhere.'

'I read about the boilers exploding during flood,' I said.

'*Si, terribile.* The oil ruined everything.'

Making sympathetic noises, I stared at the large mole beside the narrator's mouth, out of which dangled two dark hairs like the barbels of a catfish. I was seized by an intolerable longing for a shower and a change of clothes, and the moment a new arrival claimed the signora's attention I took the lift up to my room.

The trattoria, where the padrone and his wife, assisted by other members of his family, served an all-Italian clientele, promised good local fare that night. I ordered a carafe of Chianti and, for a starter Italian-style, a pasta dish followed by my favourite *pollo al pomodoro*. Calorie-conscious as I am, I skipped the dessert and had a cup of black coffee to round off the meal.

I should have been tired after the day's travelling, and with the wine flowing pleasurably in my veins. Instead, I felt my perceptions heightened. Like an explorer setting foot on a virgin island, I recorded the sights and sounds around me:

Italian voices, diners tucking heartily into their food. In between mouthfuls or sips of wine, they talked animatedly, now and again airing a loud laugh or greeting friends with southern exuberance. From the nearby kitchen issued the unobtrusive clanking of pots and pans, and the smell of cooking.

Amid such agreeable goings-on, the padrone acted his part. A king in turned-up shirt sleeves, he offered a profuse welcome to newcomers, arranged tables, took orders and supervised the waiter. In quieter moments he meandered past tables, visibly enjoying the expressions of culinary anticipation or contentment on his patrons' faces. '*E bene, signor, signora?*' With a curt bow he would acknowledge a compliment as to the excellence of a particular dish, before refilling a glass or swinging a large napkin into action, if only to remove an offensive breadcrumb. When asked for the bill, he moved with the discretion of a four-star head-waiter. To patrons known to him, he presented it with a studied air of remoteness, which suggested that charging regular diners for their meal was something degrading, if regretfully necessary. And he did not fail to observe certain niceties, while he gathered his lire. Were the bambini getting on well in school? Was the signora's leg on the mend? . . .

Nothing had changed, I mused when it came to the locals eating out at a family-run restaurant. I felt in high spirits. I was back in my beloved Florence and, for an hour or two, close to the pulse of its people. Surely, I had got off to a good start.

It had stopped raining when I walked back to the hotel, and street lanterns were spreading a hazy light. Pressing my handbag to my body, and keeping well to the centre of the pavement, I tried to avoid eye-contact with strolling males, and with *signori* loitering in dark hallways, several of whom breathed explicit propositions at *'La bella signora'*. And when, by way of an overture, one bobbed out of his lair, to wish the lone lady a 'Buona sera', I quickened my gait. Yet, if I was honest, I experienced no displeasure at such pesterings. On the contrary, I was conscious of a sudden spring in my step.

Perhaps the sensation ought to have acted as a warning.

Memory, by some trick or higher authoritative command, will often religiously preserve some events in our lives, vividly recalling certain landscapes, faces or emotions at will, while not resisting Time to obfuscate or totally erase others. Mine celebrated an orgy that night.

Tired as I was, sleep evaded me. My mattress, it seemed, had turned into hard wooden slats. With its window closed, the room felt airless; while, if I left it open, even an inch, the noise of nocturnal traffic cleaved into my wakefulness. I switched the air-conditioner on, but quickly turned it off again, when the ceiling grill emitted lukewarm air laced with what nauseatingly smelt like perfumed insect spray. Pools of perspiration formed in the clefts and hollows of my body, a clammy veil covered my face. I took the blanket off, finally my nightdress. As the darkness thickened around me, the goblins of the past crept stealthily back into the folds of my mind. They lifted the sheet and stroked my body. They made me feel deliciously, achingly young . . .

* * *

Paolo and I met on the Ponte Vecchio in the spring of sixty-six.

Ours was the kind of encounter that is often seen as a whim of fate, as pre-ordained or simply as a matter of chance. I often wondered whether a broken bra-strap or some similar mishap that morning, my lingering in front of a shop window or any other caprice of the spirit, might have prevented us from meeting in the same spot at the same time.

I was watching the sunset from under one of the arches that break up the row of jewellers' and goldsmiths' shops on the famous bridge. Before me, a striking scene: an orange-coloured sun injecting flaming streaks of light into the sluggish green waters of the river Arno, and bathing the roof-tops, turrets and domes in a soft rosy haze, thus mellowing or suffusing their outlines.

Behind me, hawkers were selling postcards and cheap Michelangelo prints to tourists. A group of boisterous Americans were drawling Texas vowels and taking up camera positions. From the Lungarno, the drone of traffic reached vexingly over the water. Suddenly, all sound filtered out of my consciousness. In a world of my own, the centuries receded. I thought of the great masters of the Renaissance, who had made Florence a mecca of art and architecture. Of the poets and scribes who had once stood on the Ponte Vecchio at sunset like myself, marvelling at the blushing of the city at the close of day, or seeking creative inspiration. Perhaps Dante had once leaned on the same parapet, gazing at all this rosiness and the softness of contours, whilst shaping in his mind new immortal lines for *La Vita Nova*. Or Byron. Or . . .

A male voice, warm and deep, catapulted me back to the present in heavily accentuated English.

'A beautiful sunset, signorina, isn't it?'

I looked at a tall young man in his late twenties, and I liked what I saw: classical features, curly brown hair and blue eyes, an inoffensive smile which displayed a generous mouth and immaculate teeth. Our eyes met, looked on and boldly scanned each other's face.

'*E molto bello,*' I replied, conscious of a sense of wonder welling up inside me. And like a seismograph, my nerve endings told me that the gods were heaping fair weather on me. For with the same certainty, with which in the past my appendix scar had faithfully forecast an approaching thunder storm or a steadily intensifying atmospheric depression, I knew that forthwith Florence would no longer be a mere custodian of art for me, no longer just a repository of artefacts and a paragon of visual delights.

As a gentle breeze winged itself through the arches of the bridge and between our mesmerized faces, I also realised that what was happening between me and this handsome stranger was love at first sight, a phenomenon so often clichéd and fictionalised, yet so seldom experienced in real life in its most startling manifestation – the attraction of matching body chemistry engendering an explosion of the senses.

As dusk fell we walked off the Ponte together. Over an espresso and apéritivo, and later over dinner in a cosy ristorante, we talked about ourselves, shamelessly exploring each other's mind, as if hoping not to find a convergence of spirits, but rather ideas alien to the other's sensibilities – something, anything that would dam the spring-tide of our emotions. The discovery that we shared a passion for Florence's Quattro- and Quintocento finally tore down the flood barriers. Our hands touched as if by accident, and they did not recoil. I felt a high-voltage current sweeping through me, reaching my vitals, while my brain desperately tried not to fuse.

As we saw our feelings mirrored in each other's eyes, our talk slowed down. Long before our glasses were empty, we knew that we had passed through a secret gate into an enchanted garden, curious like children, marvelling like adults.

'Shall we go?' Paolo asked, and took my arm. No more. Silently we walked out into a clear spring night in which a modicum of peace had descended over the city, and the air was suffused with the scent of pine and plum blossom wafting down from the hills.

Paolo, an arts graduate, backpacking globetrotter and accomplished gold- and silversmith, worked in his grandfather's exclusive shop on the Ponte Vecchio where, in the fourteenth century, the city's esteemed trade had first set up business in miniature houses and workshops along the bridge, some of which projected over the Arno, often graced with tiny, flower-potted balconies.

Since the death of his parents in a road accident a few years earlier, Paolo was living in their town flat among a curious conglomeration of inherited antique furniture and fine paintings, and the kind of objects with which a young bachelor of means and modern tastes will surround himself, all too often without becoming a slave to proud housekeeping.

I remember my first visit: a pair of jeans hanging over a bow-legged chair in the sitting-room, a stack of papers languishing on an ornate sideboard between a silver angel and a Murano vase; a polished table scattered with dog-eared paperbacks, a motoring magazine, a pair of sunglasses, the unfinished charcoal drawing of a nude, and a glass containing dregs of red wine. And jumping from the window-sill, eyeing me with the hauteur of a queen, before according me her favour by rubbing her back elegantly against my leg, was Sarah, Paolo's white feline companion.

In the kitchen, among the ubiquitous trappings of Italian cooking, I spotted a plate with the dried remains of a meal, an array of bottles, a basket bulging with onions, tomatoes and peppers, sticks of pasta and a string of garlic. In a corner, T-shirts waiting to be laundered, on the window-sill a wilting geranium. Details sketched in my memory, and perhaps most distinctly of the bedroom: the large unmade bed with its fine pin-striped sheets, a black-and-white striped bathrobe, lamps both ultra-modern and expensively antique. On the wall, a crucifix – Jesus in solid silver nailed to an ebony cross, a poster advertising an international silver- and goldsmiths' fair. On the dressing table, among other male paraphernalia, one of Paolo's own creations – a miniature silver version of Florence's famous porcellino, the copper boar which, with its rub-my-nose-for-luck snout, had delighted tourists for centuries.

Above all, I remember the fierce summer sun drumming on the flat roof above, and the bedroom retaining much of the day's heat. Or moonlight refracted through the shutters and forming slabs on the walls, the light of dawn shaping its own silhouettes. And beside me, Paolo breathing softly, an arm slung possessively across my chest. A feeling, deep down, as if my body were bedded on cotton wool, on rose petals, on air cushions. My sleep-heavy, floating morning thoughts being drawn to my lover's dreams . . .

Outside, the streets had quietened down. Cars were passing at less frequent intervals, fewer motorcycles tore the night explosively apart. And now more sweetmeat memories stole into my wakefulness: Viareggio, the Versilian seaside resort. A beach not yet packed with noisome tourists or plagued by tattooed, beer-drinking youths, still free of topless sunbathers and commercial molestation. A beach where one could still hear the waves lapping ashore, and where soft talk did not yet drown in the blare of transistor radios.

July temperatures were bearing down on Florence. Creeping through the narrow, airless streets, which were blistering in the midday sun, giant Pullman coaches were belching poisonous fumes that found no upward drift. Over the torpid river the heat hung like a soaked blanket. Tourists, however, were not deterred by the swelter. Sun-hatted and camera-slung, they were still tramping around the city in droves, eyes wide, voices high with Baedeker-guided appreciation or merely a sense of wonder. But now many of the elderly packaged sight-seers could be seen, pausing on stone or marble steps, or seeking the coolness of a church.

As the heat continued, I felt inertia invading my body like a virus. And it was not long before my studies suffered and I thought of excuses to put down my pen or postpone a visit to the Biblioteka or one of the museums.

'Let's get away from this hot-house for a while,' said Paolo one morning. An hour later his Fiat whisked us away from the oppressive city.

On Viareggio beach Paolo's appearance caused furore among the female holiday-makers, whose indiscreet stares would follow him whenever he was passing by in his black swimming trunks, tall, narrow-hipped and broad-shouldered, a man sure of himself, who did not seek his reflection in women's eyes, or flaunt his maleness paparozzi fashion . . .

How keenly, in the wasteland of the night, my mind was relaying images freed of the static interference of the years; how vividly the sounds and smells came back. Now my inner eye turned to the wisteria-clad trattoria which nestled against pine trees at one end of the beach, drawing the coolness of their shade in daytime, while creating a romantic vantage point for spectacular sunsets, or for magic nights whenever a crescent or full moon was dripping liquid silver on to the sea.

My memory released the combined perfume of jasmine, bougainvillae and wisteria drifting down from villa gardens, the sound of a mandolin, the tenor voice which a seaward breeze would carry right down to the edge of the water.

Walking barefoot by the sea in the late hours, we had stepped on tiny sea shells which tickled our feet and made us squeal like children. And the moon found no clouds behind which to hide, whenever we stretched out on the deserted beach, where the warm sand had an hour-glass quality. Where we were alone with our sweet whisperings, the soft swell of the sea and the chirping of the cicadas.

How gentle Paolo's hands had been – the hands of an artisan used to working silver and gold into delicate items of bijouterie, and to fondling prized objects, rather than finger them with proprietorial greed . . .

Here, I believe, I fell asleep, a smile tracing my lips, my skin aglow, my arms and legs cruciform under the sheet.

I woke late next morning, a sated dream still lingering about me, a smile still etched around the corners of my mouth. I reminded myself that my plan required a disciplined, detached attitude, and that nostalgia for the passions of one's youth was a sure sign of approaching middle age. But somehow such self-scolding did not work. For when I stepped out of the shower, I viewed my naked body in the full-length mirror. My hands cupped my breasts, they folded over my stomach, stroked the promontories of my hip and descended to the silky triangle between my thighs. I felt absurdly pleased with my rekindled sensuality, with a body which in its high summer was experiencing a spring tide.

Nervously I played with my hair. Light brown in colour, and having lost little of its shine over the years, it was still keeping those treacherous grey harbingers of advancing age at bay. I wished, however, it were styled more softly and with some concession to its natural waves.

While I was dressing, I realised that my mood was at odds with the formality of my suit. Why, I asked myself, had I not packed my cheeky Chanel two-piece, which always produced, if temporarily, a sparkle in Charles' eyes? With a sudden recklessness I shifted a strand of hair to fall over the side of my forehead, pertly, like an unruly lock. In the same spirit I undid the top buttons of my blouse, aiming at a more casual effect.

'A slight disorder in the dress / kindles in clothes a certain wantonness . . . ' I recited to my modified mirror image, grinning. I thought the poet Robert Herrick could not have expressed my subconscious design more succinctly, whereupon I applied some blusher to my cheeks and got busy with lipstick and eyeliner.

As I took the lift down to the breakfast room, I felt like a schoolgirl about to throw herself into the adventure of another day.

I was ready for my first assignment.

4

I don't know if I could have altered the course of events, if I had made straight for the Ponte Vecchio that morning, or to any of the places I had marked for my professional visit, thinking of nothing but the job ahead. If, on reaching the Loggia end of the Piazza St Maria Novella, my mind had not strayed to Ucello's fresco 'The Deluge' in the Choistro Verde, the cloister adjoining the striking mosaic facade of the church at the other end of the square. If, ultimately, the sun had not been close to her zenith in an unseasonably clear November sky.

But retrospective conjectures are only an interesting pastime. They itch the playful mind with hypotheses. They serve no purpose other than adding spice to a debating point. For they change or reverse nothing.

I recalled my professor's advice: 'You need good light for the fresco. Best time is just before noon on a sunny day.' I wondered how good a job the restorers had made of the famous painting which had been among the artefacts severely damaged by the flood. I suddenly saw a thematic opener for my journalistic assessment of the city's restoration work: the biblical deluge, as depicted in all its horrors by the artist's fourteenth-century imagination and, in a wider sense, begging a parallel with the city's devastating flood of modern times. It also occurred to me that the rising waters and the raging storm, so vividly portrayed in the fresco, formed a coincidental comparison with my own emotional state.

I headed towards the cloister.

I saw her from afar. Standing in front of the sun-lit church, feeding an army of blackish pigeons, the Lady in Grey was so absorbed in her ministrations that she was totally oblivious of a group of Japanese tourists clicking their cameras for a close-up of the church, with herself and the pigeons in the foreground. I decided to leave her in communion with the birds and walked down the stone steps to the low-lying cloister.

'We'll soon be closing for lunch, signora,' the uniformed attendant informed me; a bald, square-faced and thick-set man who bore an uncanny resemblance to Mussolini. As he handed me a ticket, 'Il Duce' bared a row of ultra-white teeth.

The pillared quadrangle, in the midst of which four obelisk-shaped cypresses gently rocked against the blue sky, was ill-served by the November sun. But although no more than twilight prevailed along its western walls, it was vibrant with peacefulness. By shutting out the bustle and cacophony of the square, the archways and the grassed inner courtyard welcomed the visitor with a serenity that opened up avenues of inner space.

I sat down on the parapet opposite Ucello's fresco – two scenes of the ark conceived as a double vision and united in a singular scheme. The colours had faded over the centuries, and some of the details had been so ravished by the foul waters of sixty-six that some incidents were no longer clear. Although I was familiar with the geometry Ucello had applied to his fresco, just as I was with the profusion of figures and animals caught up in the fury of the elements, as a means to heighten the drama of the Deluge, I was not prepared for the subtleties of my emotions. More than ever I was stirred by the copious composition and the artist's scientific approach to perspective. And with nothing more than bridgeable space between myself and the fresco, I experienced the same thrill of immediacy which, in the past, paintings capable of arresting my imagination, and inviting my empathy, had aroused in me.

As if I were viewing the tableau of violence for the first time, my eyes fixed on the horrors of the biblical cataclysm as brought to life by the master's forceful vision.

Against a backcloth of swirling waters, flashes of lightning and trees twisting under the power of the tempest, death, human despair and selfishness is crowding around the ark. A crow pecks out the eyes of a dead man, the belly of a drowned child arches up like a balloon; arms and legs are lashing out in their fight to gain a hold on the narrow ledge of the ark. The water is slapping against the bows, the wind is howling. And now I am one of the screaming, beseeching multitude. Treading water, I search for floating objects that might serve as islands of survival. Around me, bloated bodies are surfacing; faces, eyes wide with terror, disappear like weighted bags. On the meagre ledge of the steep bulkhead, which is tightly sealed, men are brandishing sticks to secure, or defend, their temporary foothold. I swallow water, as the arms of a strong swimmer thrash out and propel themselves towards the ark which is riding high on the current. But now a drowning woman grabs my thigh, holds it in a vice, pulls me under. A last spark of lightning illuminates the savage scene, sears my eyes, before my lungs fill with water.

I am sinking as rapidly as if my ankles were chained to a prisoner's iron ball. Around me, the water is alive with the convulsive twitching of the drowning, and with the cruciform floating bodies of the drowned. Deeper and deeper I plummet, to where the water is black and lifeless. To where a current of monstrous velocity seizes me and painfully sucks me down a narrow shaft. I feel sickened by the speed of my descent, my brain is gyrating, squeezing out a last thought: This is what it must be like, to be plunging from a skyscraper to one's death, a human bomb which, seconds later, will leave nothing on the pavement below but a mess of broken bones, blood and grey matter.

But now my fall breaks, as if a parachute on my back had opened. The shaft grows wider, its walls translucent. Dove-grey light unfolds before me, pillars and arches drift into focus. My thighs register the chill of stone. My stomach is aware of a fairground sensation – the hated after-effect of riding 'The Flying Wheel' or 'The Big Dipper' as a child. In my ears there is the echo of a howling gale, of water smacking against a solid object – sounds which are led by a fiendish human choir. Out of such cacophony a firm male voice rises and establishes itself:

'We're closing, signorina.'

I stared at an angular face, a receding hairline and a prominent chin. A mean-lipped mouth, whose teeth showed signs of dental neglect, now spelled out the words:

'We–are–closing, signorina.'

Greedily, my lungs sucked in air.

'Who are you?' I asked the young man in uniform.

'*Il custode*, signorina.'

Why was he calling me 'signorina'? I wondered. Was he trying to charm a tip out of me? And where exactly was I? But then, behind him, barely discernible, I caught sight of Noah looking up at a hovering image of God. The fresco. The Green Cloister. Like the last puzzle-piece, reality put itself into place and memory returned.

'*Va bene*, signorina?' inquired the figure of minor authority, who looked the younger image of the former fascist dictator.

'*Si, si, gracie*,' I replied, and I was about to rise, when my eyes fell on the clothes I was wearing. Instantly, my restored sense of orientation turned into a state of panic and disbelief. My pulse quickened as from an overdose of amphetamine.

In the young man, my terrified expression must have elicited anxiety, for he repeated, '*Va bene?*'

'*Si, si*,' I cried, and although deep in the abyss of shock and speculations, I shot to my feet. Surely, I thought, this was something out of science fiction. Not only had I brought to life Ucello's visual concept of the biblical flood, but a weird force of energy had drawn me physically into the depicted scene of horror, before sluicing me through a vertical nightmare back to a reality which saw me wearing an outfit from my casual student days: soft-soled, low-heeled shoes, corduroy trousers, a T-shirt and an all-purpose anorak. Where was my smart shoulder-strap hand-bag, my designer-cut suit? And why had the light suddenly drained out of the quadrangle, when – what seemed only minutes ago, the sky over Florence had been cloudless? Perhaps I was still dreaming? Perhaps fever fantasies were racking my brain, and any moment now I would be waking up in a hospital bed? Or, still worse, had I turned insane?

'Signorina!' The attendant rattled his keys for emphasis.

A last glance through the ashen light at 'The Deluge', the washed-out colours and blurred contours of which struck me as incapable of befuddling the senses. With a gigantic effort I walked towards the exit.

'Don't forget your *bagaglio*,' the attendant shouted after me. He picked up a tightly-packed canvas bag by its straps and handed it to me.

'*Gracie.*' With undisguised reluctance I accepted a backpack that seemed not entirely unfamiliar and weighed a ton.

'Where's the other man who let me in?' I asked. 'I mean, the older one?'

The chap looked dumbfounded. 'There's only me, signorina. At this time of the year it's only me. Not too many people find their way into the cloisters, anyway.'

He quickly shut the wrought-iron gate and turned away. His siesta beckoned.

5

A gloomy sky hung over the piazza. Although a steady drizzle was freeing it from sightseers and strollers, its western end was still throbbing with traffic, and the pigeons still formed a moving carpet in front of the church.

There was no sign of the Lady in Grey.

The first shop window returned my image, and the person I saw was slim and wore her hair long, clasped at the back into a ponytail. My fingers reached out, touched and recoiled. By now startled bats were fluttering in my guts, my heart pounded uncomfortably and my legs moved like stilts. Don't lose your head, commanded my grey cells. Get yourself a newspaper and find out the month and year you've landed yourself in.

I hastened to the nearest news-stand. But what about money? Where did I – no, do I – keep my change? Questions that seemed to be utterly superfluous, for how could I have forgotten! Hovering between tears and the sharp edge of excitement, I went through my button-through anorak pocket, which yielded lire, a passport and a train ticket.

I asked for a paper.

'*Quello giornale?*'

'Any morning paper,' I cried, 'I don't mind.'

The news vendor stared at me, as I tore a mass-circulation daily out of her hand and my eyes devoured the date.

It was the second of November, nineteen hundred and sixty-six.

For as long as it takes to study the profile of a new situation, I stood rooted to the ground. I licked the rain off my lips and shifted the straps of my pack, which were cutting into my shoulders. Stupified, looking straight through oncoming pedestrians who had to navigate their way past me on the narrow pavement like a river round a rocky obstacle, I finally stumbled ahead.

I shall have to keep my wits about me, I told myself, as the extent of my plight took shape. Somehow I had got myself involved in a time warp. Real fiction stuff this. A Wellsian adventure of the most fantastic order. For here I was, forty-three years old, yet I didn't have to consult my passport to confirm the disparity in age. I knew I looked like a twenty-three-year-old; I knew that I was pretty. But I was also a married woman and the mother of a grown-up son, whose mature reasoning powers were unimpaired. The realisation that twenty years of adult living were locked up within me was awesome. Ludicrous, however, was the fact that I was capable of remembering what I had had for breakfast before I left for the airport, and what for dinner at the trattoria last night. I recalled the coach trip from Pisa to Florence, and the 'Grey Lady' being the subject of my guessing game. And equally vivid: my plan to drive Paolo – whether by direct confrontation or some dirty trick of the imagination – into an arid hinterland of my mind, from where there led no road back.

I need a coffee, I thought; strong, black and no sugar.

As I sipped the hot liquid at the nearest coffee bar, I

tried to reshuffle my thoughts and plan my next step. In the absence of guide-lines for the reversal of time shifts, I knew I would have to depend on my wits and – how frightful an idea – wait around until I found the operative medium, But first of all I ought to go back to the hotel, test my identity and the fabric of this Kafkaesque metamorphosis.

The sight of the hotel's grim, if noble, façade momentarily restored my equanimity. But as soon as I entered the lobby, I realised that there was little hope I would be given my room key. For a vaulted stuccoed ceiling and gilt-framed paintings looked down on fifteenth- and sixteenth-century furniture; and rugs, Persian and well-trodden, covered the marble floor.

'Can I help you?' asked a raven-haired, dark-eyed woman in her late twenties from behind a reception desk, scanning my appearance like a grand-hotel commissionaire.

'May I have my key, please,' I said, without blinking. 'Number Five.'

The woman looked at the keyboard, then consulted a book. 'A gentleman is staying in Number Five. Are you sure . . . When did you arrive? I can't remember registering you.'

By now any pretence of politeness towards *la inglesa* had gone, and her arched eyebrows suggested that any pack-carrying young woman wearing my kind of outfit, and asking for the key of an occupied room, when she was not actually staying at the hotel, was bound to have criminal or immoral intentions.

Stammering something about having got the wrong hotel, I glanced at the large mole beside the woman's mouth, which sprouted two black hairs. And it was no consolation that on my hurried way out my eyes fell on a gilt-framed octagonal Florentine mirror which hung as proudly between two paintings of the Veronese school as between two equals.

Back in the street, I dumped my pack in a doorway and leaned against the wall. Never before had I been forced to admit utter helplessness. My courage felt battered, my sense of forlornness was acute. I appealed to my faculties of reasoning, I prayed for a spark of higher intelligence that would allow me to find my way back into my own time.

I recalled two incidents during my student days and one not so long ago, when the depth of visual experience had temporarily detached my mind from reality. When paintings – perhaps due to an unusual receptiveness of my brain at the time – had been more than lifeless canvases: Salvador Dali's 'St John on the Cross', Joseph Barber's 'Landscape to a Golden Age' and John Hunter's 'Good Night to Skye' – paintings which, centuries removed from my own study genre, had affected me so powerfully that I appeared to have literally stepped into the framed scenes.

During such experiences I had totally cut myself off from the hushed silence of other gallery visitors and the clicking sound of ladies' heels on the parquet flooring – even from the clatter of cups and saucers in the adjacent cafeteria. A physical presence in Dali's awe-inspiring cosmic dream on the shore of Lake Genezareth, I had looked up at the crucified Christ on a cross suspended at a daring angle under dramatic lighting; I stood with an urban escapist's enchantment on Hunter's rocky beach, watching the light falling over the Isle of Skye, and listening to the cries of the seagulls; I rested my stressed psyche in Barber's depiction of an Edenic landscape. But intense as each experience had been, I had always returned from such empathic sorties as to the snap of a finger and with the laws of Time remaining unaffected. Indeed, I had stepped out of the artist's panorama and back into a more tangible world as facilely as through a door.

By now I was certain that it was the intensity with which I had allowed my imagination to project itself visually into Ucello's portrayal of the biblical deluge, which had brought the time leap about. I decided to go back to the cloister in the afternoon and, by forcing an equally intense confrontation, use the fresco as a catalyst, to return to my own time. But immediately, the art expert in me rejected the idea. The light, I knew, would be too poor to recognise any details. And now, through a mesh curtain of rain, I stared at the sombre sky as if it had defrauded me. But no fracture, no thinning of the clouds, promised a timely brightening up.

Out of curiosity, and in order to give my brain time to devise another course of action, I examined the rest of my pockets. A man-sized handkerchief, a roll of mints, a cinema ticket, a pocket comb, a lipstick, a butcher's receipt and a piece of polished, marble-sized Carrera rock came to light. A small zipped inside pocket finally produced a door-key on a metal ring.

The last find took my breath away, for it opened up wild and titillating possibilities which, for lack of a saner, effective alternative, beckoned to be explored.

Still dazed, deaf to the din of traffic, and weary of Vespas darting past and around obstacles in the road like minnows, I walked through the corridors of wet streets and alleys that seemed to lead me farther away from the future. I needed no street-plan, for all the landmarks were still *in situ*. Here and there, more intimate recognition dawned: a landscape painting in an antiquarian's window, reminiscent of Ruisdal's chromatic melancholy – clouds, ominous and moody, shifting light and shade and, in places, lighting up a patch of water, field or marsh; a grocer's window, in which garlic bulbs and plastic tomatoes were strung up to make a decorative garland; a pasta factory, where through a glass panel shoppers could watch dough being hand-rolled, cut or twirled into assorted noodle shapes. Or the red silk blouse in the Roman boutique, which had me wondering every time I passed whether I would ever be able to afford clothes with a designer label.

At the sight of the three-storey building my legs began to wobble and my mouth thirsted for a long drink. Clay-coloured, here and there exhibiting touches of former ochre tones, flat-roofed, and its windows corniced and shuttered, it was one of the many old Florentine town houses which had retained a faint aura of gentility, notwithstanding the fact that over the years they had seen shops and small workshops moving into their ground-floors and basements.

A brass-knobbed door led into a hallway which smelt musty, and whose whitewashed walls were badly in need of a new coat of paint. Dragging myself upstairs, my mind, suddenly alert to the venture ahead, issued conflicting messages: There's still time to turn back, it said. But where would I go? Where else could I go? As I approached the top-floor flat, a wave of excitement rolled through my trunk, warm and wanton. My hand trembled as it inserted the key in the lock.

It fitted.

I experienced an instant sense of familiarity, of objects being still in the same places, and rooms testifying to their recent occupation. Memories rose out of every chair. They were sitting around the kitchen table and lounging in the living-room. In the bedroom, injecting sweet poison under my epidermis, they jumped eagerly at me from under the crumpled sheets. Yet, somehow, everything seemed to be on a different scale.

Prodigal sons and daughters returning to their father's house must feel like this, I thought. Or, in the days when all that had wings in the air were birds, travellers coming home after many years of sojourn through distant continents: the reduction of dimensions, the fading of colours. Thus it was for me now. The rooms looked smaller and, in the mean light, dusty and lustreless. Even the cobalt-blue hyacinth, which I had bought a few days prior to my departure, appeared to have paled.

A hissing noise behind me startled me. Sarah, the white cat, which had graciously bestowed her affections on me when I moved in with her provider, stood at a respectable distance, arching her back and shooting at me green darts of cold dislike from behind half-closed lids.

'Sarah,' I crooned, venturing forward, to stroke and calm her aggressive back. But the cat, still hissing, inched backward and sought refuge under an armchair.

But there was no time to ponder feline fickleness. Realising Paolo would soon be home for lunch, I got busy. I tore up the farewell note which still leant mockingly against a bottle of vinegar on the kitchen table, and flashed the fragments down the toilet. I chopped vegetables for a *sopa verdura* and brought a pot of water to the boil for pasta. I set the table and unpacked.

I moved as under hypnosis, mind and limbs performing but perfunctorily, and not until I went into the bathroom, to stick my toothbrush into the rack next to Paolo's, did my mind unblock. I remembered Charles' toothbrush leaning drunkenly against the rim of a glass on his side of our large, marble-topped wash-basin. Briefly, the juxtaposition of images generated a feeling of acute anguish, as well as frustration at my farcical situation. Like an inebriate trying to chill herself into sobriety, I liberally splashed cold water on my face. And now my mirror image made my younger self take on the commanding role. I ran my fingers over my cheeks and lips, wondrous, yet still distrustful of their suppleness, helpless against the slow smile that was stealing over my face.

Then I curled up in an armchair, tense but acquiescent. I realised that in the absence of a magic wand, with which to rocket myself forward in time, I had no alternative but to give my mind a rest, not only from attempting to disentangle past, present and future, but also from computing my chances to re-enter my former orbit.

Uncanny, brain-racking as things might be, they required a temporary acceptance. I hated to admit, of course, that such a policy conveniently unshackled me from moral arguments. It gave me a passport to licence.

6

In all the years I have been married to Charles I have never slept with another man, nor felt tempted to taste the proverbially forbidden and supposedly sweeter fruit growing in another man's orchard. Admittedly, my mind had lately coveted adulterous pleasures, but a sense of guilt had always edged itself between my unchaste thoughts and my conscience.

Now, as the door opened, and I set eyes on Paolo again, my heart pounded shamelessly and every fibre in my body ached with a longing that overrode the last timorous stirring of moral scruples.

I smiled at my lover.

'Ciao, Claire. I came as soon as I could. What time did you say your train was leaving?'

The voice. The eyes. That gorgeous figure of a man! How could I have insulted his image with the ravages the years might have heaped upon him? How could I have wanted to soil it with crude assumptions and speculations, in order to rid myself of his virile ghost?

'*Eh, chiara*, what's the matter? Lost your voice?' As Paolo came over and kissed me, I felt all the fountains within me breaking up.

'What time is your train leaving?' he repeated, his face

suddenly funereal, his buoyancy crumbling.

'I . . . I decided to . . . to stay on for a while,' I stammered, the lie spuming from my lips.

Paolo beamed. His arms were around me.

'That's wonderful, darling. What made you change your mind?'

My explanation, evasively bland and not given to further scrutiny, must have sounded plausible enough, for it reaped me an instant reward. Paolo, exploding with boyish delight, pulled me to my feet and whirled me around the room as in an exhibitionist rock-and-roll dance routine. And, finally, holding me tight, 'We must celebrate tonight, Clairissima. I feel like a condemned man who's been given a reprieve.' He looked around. 'Where's Sarah?'

'Under the chair.'

A gleam of greenish yellow revealed the cat's whereabouts. 'What's she doing there?'

'I don't know,' I said. 'She's not been very friendly this last hour.'

Paolo called the cat and coaxed her out of her hiding place. 'Eh, what's got into you?'

The cat looked at me, hostility in her stance and hissing like a steam engine. Not letting me out of her sight, she stalked over to Paolo and brushed her coat briefly against his trouser leg, before swiftly repairing to her new hide-out.

Paolo looked worried.

'I hope she isn't ill. You know how she loves sitting on the window-sill during the day.'

I took flight in the mundane.

'Lunch will be ready soon,' I said, and nipped into the kitchen, where I busied myself, stirring, forking, cutting and ladling. I felt like jumping on a trampoline.

* * *

Although I was ravenous, eating turned out to be no more than a process of masticating and swallowing, the latter assisted by frequent gulps of wine. Act normal, I told myself. Try and divest yourself of your maturity in speech and mannerisms. In short, try and behave and sound like a twenty-three-year-old.

I sneered at my self-counsel. Play-acting had never been my forte, yet the role into which I had manoeuvred myself required a perfect performance. One with a difference. For while a professional actress, whose years normally cast her in character parts, might sometimes have to play a youthful heroine on stage, the curtain will always come down for her. At the end of the last act, freed of make-believe make-up, she sheds the Thespian's accoutrements of youth and re-attunes mentally and in the way she dresses to her age.

In contrast, my act guaranteed no foreseeable final curtain, and it encumbered me with a two-level consciousness which I knew I would find impossible to sustain synchronically for long.

'You're very quiet, Claire,' remarked Paolo, breaking off a chunk of bread. 'You're not regretting your decision to stay on, I hope?'

'Of course not.' I flashed a young Claire's smile at him and fleetingly touched his hand. 'I've had a hell of a headache all morning. It must be the weather.'

As I looked at the rain-splashed kitchen window, a sudden vision struck me so forcefully that I dropped my spoon. I had been so busy, trying to come to terms with my physical and emotional entrapment, and with working out this new dimension of time, which required an updated definition of reality, that I had failed to look ahead at the impending disaster and the fate that would befall Florence in about thirty-six hours. And so violent was my reaction to this history-based foreknowledge that I jumped up and went to the window.

'*Que cosa*, Claire?' Paolo sounded worried.

Across the wet roofs and through a coalescence of grey hues I glimpsed a stretch of the lacklustre river. In a voice that winged eerily through the kitchen I said:

'The river will swell and break over the Lungarno, swamping all the low-lying areas of the city the day after tomorrow . . . in the early hours of the morning. In some places the water will be rising to ten, twelve feet and more . . . '

'Stop it, Claire,' cried Paolo. 'You sound like a clairvoyant — no, more like a phoney crystal-ball gazer.'

'I'm not joking,' I countered, while my face was already in mourning for Cimabue's famous crucifix, and for a multitude of other invaluable artefacts revered by art lovers the world over. And for the thousands of books, ancient manuscripts and antiques which I knew were going to be ravished by the worst flood since Michelangelo's time. And Ucello's fresco . . . My heart missed a beat, as I realised the implications. 'Believe me,' I said, 'I sometimes have the gift of precognition.'

'If you're not joking, then you're letting pessimism get the better of you,' said Paolo. 'Remember, the Arno has often risen dangerously after a heavy rainfall in the past, without causing flooding. Come, *chiara*, finish your lunch. I don't like you playing Cassandra.'

But my mood would not lift, nor the rain stop.

Paolo made coffee. He put a sugar bowl in front of me, and was about to pour warm milk into my cup, crooning, 'One cappuccino coming up, signorina,' when I intervened.

'No milk, no sugar,' I said, waving my hand as if to drive away a troublesome fly. 'I like my coffee black.'

Paolo looked startled.

'Since when? You always take milk with it. You love cappuccino, and only this morning I saw you ladle two teaspoonfuls of sugar into your cup.'

I mentally pinched myself. I had slipped up. The years might have dropped from my appearance, but my idiosyncracies, including the preferences of my taste buds, acquired over twenty years, remained unaffected. Playing down my sudden fondness for *caffè nero*, if only to wipe the baffled expression off Paolo's face, I said with an impish smile:

'Oh well, I suppose women have a knack of changing their likes and dislikes unpredictably. Perhaps it's their prerogative. Did not Virgil note that woman *est varium et mutabile semper?*'

Paolo laughed:

'How right Virgil was!'

'What do you mean?'

'That woman *is* always fickle and changing! But fancy you knowing Latin!'

Another embarrassment, wholly unforeseen and more difficult to explain away than my sudden U-turn in the way I liked my coffee, was yet to come. And it was a sign of my mental preoccupation with the days ahead that only minutes after I had told myself to be wary of any further traps, I fell headlong into another. This time, I needed more plausible excuses to extract myself.

Having lit two cigarettes, Paolo offered me one, while scanning the headlines of the morning paper.

'No, thank you,' I said, still deep in the vale of my musings, 'I don't smoke.'

'What?' Paolo eyed me, as if I had declared my intention to ride à la Lady Godiva past the Palazzio Vecchio.

'What I mean is, I don't feel like it,' I hastened to add. 'In fact, I've decided to give it up.'

'Since when?'

'About an hour ago. It's a filthy habit, really, and medical research . . .'

Paolo's face was ripe with disbelief.

'Claire, *que cosa*? You are so strange today.'

'Nothing is the matter, I assure you.

But this time Paolo needed more convincing. By now, firm-lipped with convenient fabrications, I blamed the weather, a minor stomach upset, an article I had recently read on the ill-effects of smoking. And the words only died on my lips when Paolo led me into the sitting-room for a cuddle-up siesta.

'Please tell your grandfather what I told you,' I pleaded with Paolo, when he got ready to go back to work. And more urgently, 'Ask him to take his most precious items home with him tonight or tomorrow. Tell him that the river in spate will rise over the parapets, to flood the city, and that the jewellers and goldsmiths' shops on the Ponte Vecchio, facing upstream, will take the brunt of the raging current.'

For the first time I saw Paolo's brows narrow in mute anger, then his handsome face settled in an indulgent smile.

'I see the weather has really got through to you. Look, darling, let's go out for dinner tonight. You've been picking at your lunch like a sparrow. What d'you think? It'll do you good.'

My answer made him take the stairs two at the time.

As I closed the door behind him, I knew I would have to fetter my physical longing. For first there were many jobs to be done, and time was at a premium.

It was still raining steadily when I left the house, armed with several shopping bags. By now the light was fast draining out of the streets. Rivulets were spilling into the gutters and forming treacherous pools alongside, from which passing vehicles hurled sheets of water at pedestrians. Rising from the ground, and out of every hallway, nook and cranny which the sun never reached, a damp smell hung over the alleyways; caustic, miasmic.

Top of my shopping list were two pairs of tall-shafted rubber boots, as well as two pairs of rubber gloves. Soon my bags bulged with candles and matches, tinned food and milk powder, a week's supply of mineral water, bread, groceries and a small camping stove. For good measure I bought a plastic bucket. I mused about my exclusive privilege of equipping the household I had come to share again for what I knew would be a period of emergency and a prolonged cut-off from the city's electricity supply. For the siege by an enemy which would soon be running berserk through the streets, pillaging, soiling and destroying, and which would leave its visiting-card in august buildings, churches, museums, archives, shops and houses. How lonely such a privilege made me, and – with hindsight – how unjust it was!

I approached an old lady who was shuffling along the slippy pavement, a basket over her arms, her head fixed to the ground.

'*Scusi, senora.*'

I told her what I knew. 'Take my word,' I said, 'the flood will make it impossible for you to go out shopping for many days. Anyway, most of the shops in this area will have all their stocks flushed out.'

A blank stare, a shake of the head, as if the authorities ought not to let the likes of me out among the public, then the lady escaped into the nearest shop as hastily as her legs would allow.

Loaded like a lottery winner returning from a money-spending spree, I lumbered home. I hid most of my shopping where Paolo would not find it, afraid that the extreme nature of my precautions might pluck a note of disharmony between us. My head was swirling, and no wonder. Within the space of a few hours I had been hurled through time zones and faced my former lover as if no more than a morning's work had separated us. The sudden disorientation alone could surely drive a sane person into mental bedlam. But as if the weight of such experience was not enough, I was soon to be witness to a flood disaster which would make international front-page news. And the water would not go down for days, and when it did, fetid and filthy, it would have defiled Ucello's fresco, flaking off yet more colour, and smudging oil and mud over some of the crucial details of the composition, thereby making it inaccessible to the public until such a time as restoration work on it had been completed. And only then, toned-up, and in the midday light of a fine day, might it hopefully act as catalyst again.

How oppressive such knowledge was, how cruelly it highlighted my dilemma, for in the absence of an alternative time reversal mechanism I was bound to remain a prisoner of Time.

But now there loomed a prospect which suffered no intrusion from heart-rending images, and which worked on my senses like an aphrodisiac.

I had a bath and washed my hair. Naked, wet strands of hair falling to my shoulders, I stood in front of the bedroom mirror, indulging the older woman's vanity in the reflection of a slim waistline and high-pointed firm breasts. I dressed and brushed my hair, flitting around as feverishly as a teenager about to meet the school's handsomest top-former or sports-field hero for her first date. Then I waited for Paolo's Olympian smile, and for the moment that would lead us into a lavish amatory landscape.

But then my subdued moral sentinel raised a timid finger. Should I not first make sure that the life which was steadily receding in my mind was not reachable by telephone?

I dialled our London number; I tried Charles' university extension. To no avail. I might as well have played with a battery-operated toy telephone, for all the line yielded were strange static noises and the kind of morse-bleebs which fly around the world during the night.

I smiled when I replaced the receiver, but something deep inside me hated that smile.

We both had something to celebrate that evening: Paolo, the postponement of my departure; I, my chance return to the affections of my former amoroso. But while Paolo's happiness was that of a honeymooner, my own state of mind resembled one of inebriation: I was drunk with the potions my metamorphosis had put before me. Thus, savouring my reflection in Paolo's eyes, and listening to my heart-beat, I surrendered with wings outspread to a mood of sweet abandonment.

I wore my hair open, softly draping to my shoulders and complementing a black-and-white shift dress, held at the waist by a red leather belt and tightly pleated from the mid-thigh down to the knees. I also wore a beautifully crafted silver ring embellished with the open face of a rose, which Paolo had put on my finger before we went out.

'I made it for you, chiara. I meant to give it to you this afternoon as a going-away present, as a token of my love, as something that might bring you back.'

Walking home that night, we joined the crowds pouring out of cinemas, bars and restaurants. Seemingly in no hurry to repair to bed, they sauntered along the pavements, ducking under umbrellas, and seldom passing a shop window without giving it their attention. Despite the steady rain, a demonstrative holiday spirit abounded, which made light of the weather.

Perhaps Paolo and I had imbibed a little too much vino

rosso, perhaps we were trying to mask our anticipation of the evening's pending finale. For we laughed a lot and teased each other like children. We jumped over puddles and squealed when during such manoeuvres rainwater seeped from our umbrella into our collars. We kissed unashamedly in the path of strollers, and when we ventured through the ravine of a deserted alleyway, where the rain produced light-fingered instrumental sounds on the cobblestones, I joined Paolo's fine voice, albeit haltingly, in the rendering of Don Giovanni and Zerline's duet, *Lá ci darem la mano*. 'Give me your hand, your life . . . '

I felt wonderfully alive and young and recklessly free. I chuckled at my other self: at the art historian who could eloquently lecture on, say, the art of Bellini, the garden of neo-Platonism in Boticelli's 'Primavera', or on the Byzantine influence in Sienese Renaissance paintings; who could quote passages from Dante's *Paradiso* in Italian, talk cleverly about the poet's collusion with mystery, his visions and his despair. And this was her too: the wife, the mother, the lady who had good dress sense and polished pink finger nails; the gardener who planted and weeded and watered; the housewife who did not need a cookery book in order to prepare a tasty English, French or Italian dish; the Claire, ultimately, who believed in things abiding between heaven and earth, and – against all evolutional theories and occasional twinges of doubt – in a Divine presence.

But this other woman was not wanted. Not now. And as my mind reached forward to the moment when my earlier bedtime fantasies would turn deliciously real, this other woman understood that I had to deny her.

As soon as the door to Paolo's flat closed behind us, our frolicsome foreplay ceased, the last spasms of merriment died in our throats. We looked at each other the way we first had on the Ponte Vecchio: silently, listening to the tune which was composing itself between us, indifferent, all of a sudden, to the gorgeous sunset brushing liquid gold on to the river. A communion that had been instantaneous, exquisite and all-consuming.

And now our arms flung wide open towards the tidal wave which washed over us and carried us away . . .

7

I woke to the harsh, slippery sounds of morning breaking in a wet street. The rain was splashing against the shutters, through which feeble light squeezed into the room, withholding sharp contours.

My body was floating on an airbed of happiness. It was singing the glory of the morning. Beside me Paolo stirred, turned around and nestled his face between my head and shoulder. A hand chained my waist, then traced my hip across its hump right down to my thigh, before ascending the downy mound between my legs.

Once again, the waters are rising around me, clear waters, sweet to the lips and to my nakedness, waters soon turning into a broiling sea. A huge wave lifts me on to its crest and, growing into a billowing sail, carries me landwards as on Neptune's throne, before collapsing and gently beaching me on golden sands. As the waters are ebbing away, leaving but ripples to wash feebly ashore, I am basking in the warm after-glow of my climactic ride . . .

Sipping a cup of black coffee, which was all he ever had for breakfast, Paolo stood in the kitchen like Giotto's Campanile.

'Dismal weather, this,' he remarked. And, glancing at the rain-sodden sky, 'I'll take the car this morning.'

I could not take my eyes off him. A smart fawn-coloured leather jacket, toning in with the colour of his hair and eyes, added inches to his shoulders and emphasized his narrow hips. His close-shaven, scrubbed face had the morning freshness of Wordsworth's Preludian school-boy.

'By the way, darling,' he said, 'when my grandfather heard you were staying on, he asked us over for dinner tomorrow night. I said I'd ask you.'

I wrapped Paolo's dressing gown tighter around me. Should I tell him that we would not make it to the Via Riconsoli tomorrow night, and thus risk being reproached for sticking to my story of impending gloom? Should I tell him that oil-streaked torrents would be surging through the centre of the city tomorrow, turning all streets which converged on the Piazza del Duomo into swollen, non-negotiable canals? I opted for an answer that would not provoke an argument.

'I'd like to go, I said. 'I'll buy your grandmother some flowers for the big room, something bright-coloured and sweet-scented. She's so fond of flowers.'

Paolo looked pleased.

'That would be nice, chiara. And I'll get grandfather a bottle of his favourite Ruffino.' He put down his cup and came over to me. His fingers played with my hair, tracked over my cheekbones, skated over my lips. Then he kissed me as if I were a Meissen figurine.

'*Io t'amo*, Claire. I love you.'

For a long time after he was gone, the three words hovered radiantly in the room.

I turned my attention to the sky. It was still raining heavily, and the mean light seeping through the blueish-grey cloud ceiling presaged worse to come. But then, for me, they hardly mattered as harbingers of disaster, aware as I was that neither the power I had at my elbows, nor my prescient knowledge could dam a river in spate. Except in science fiction, the course of history was unchangeable, irreversible, however coveted a modification of past events might be. But was I incapable of taking even the slightest remedial action? Perhaps I was able to help Paolo's grandparents, who would be islanded in their flat as from tomorrow. And why not test the immutability of the past? If I couldn't entirely rewrite the Flood, why not at least try to somehow lessen its impact on the treasures of Florence?

I rang Paolo's grandmother. With a diplomat's cunning I told the signora what would happen, and advised her to send her daily woman for food supplies, mineral water and candles. I half expected her to react with the impatience of the scholar, or with the pique of someone who, conscious of the increased gullibility of old age, takes umbrage at having her leg pulled. Thus, her response took me by surprise.

'It's strange,' she said, 'I had a curious nightmare last night. I dreamt I was stranded on a tiny island in a storm. Around me the sea level was rising quickly. I escaped to higher ground, but the water pursued me relentlessly. As the waves began to lick my feet, I woke up in panic. Somehow it was all so real, and it took me ages to get back to sleep.'

'I think your dream confirms my prediction,' I coaxed her. 'You should take it seriously.'

'I will, Claire,' said the old lady. 'Mind you, my husband says we've had days of continuous rain before, and the river didn't break its banks. And we've had no serious flood since 1844. But if my dream did try to tell me something, and if your own forecast comes true, it doesn't bear thinking about it. *O, dio mio*, it makes me feel quite faint.'

'Then will you do as I suggested, signora?' I asked. 'And will you tell your husband? I'm afraid Paolo is treating my warning as a big joke.'

'I will, dear girl.'

As I hung up, I felt a sense of relief that I had not been given the brush-off, and that this *simpatico* old lady would not needlessly suffer in the days to come.

The Minettis occupied a spacious top floor flat in the Via Ricasoli near the duomo. Like the grey patrician-style façade of the building, its permanently shuttered street-facing windows and the heavy brass knobs on the gate, it exhibited behind its walls all the features of wealth and seclusion.

I remember my first visit to the flat: my nostrils detecting a tomb-like smell, my eyes fastening on the opulence of 'the big room' – early Florentine furniture, precious carpets and paintings in company with a profusion of silverwork, bronze, glass and marble.

This grand dining-cum-living room, in which a life-sized bronze cast of Cellini's Perseus in his victorious posture claimed the best part of one corner, was dominated by a spectacular Murano chandelier. On an ancient oak dining-table of banquet length, heavy silverware, arranged as centre-pieces, gleamed in the sparkle of a thousand crystals. Except for two throne-sized cushioned seats, chairs were high-backed, carved and uncomfortable. The marble floor, where not covered with rugs, exposed intricate mosaic stonework. On one side of the room a glass case contained some of the daintiest items of silver craft I had ever seen – objects, I estimated, not without a touch of malice – which would lose their aura of sterility, if prised from their cage and displayed to the public eye.

Other artefacts cried out to be noticed: two vases, one Ming, the other dating back to the reign of Lorenzo di

Magnifico, both raised imperially on rosewood pedestals and devoid of flowers. And equally aloof, bronze busts, a silver eagle with outstretched wings, as well as various collectors' pieces of marble.

A magnificent room. A cold room. A room which elicited the appreciation of the art-loving visitor. But, like the other rooms of the flat, to which I had been allowed access, it did not make for cosiness around the hearth.

Signora Minetti, a former university lecturer in German studies, was white-haired and bespectacled. Despite her failing eyesight and a painful condition of her back, she still spent many hours a day in her study, a ponderous wood-panelled chamber filled with bronze statues and bookshelves. Shown around the flat during my first visit, I noticed a book-marked copy of *Faust* in German on her desk, which intimated not only scholarly interest, but linguistic excellence.

'Goethe's greatest work,' she said, eyes sparkling, 'and if you read it carefully, a treasure chest of worldly wisdom. How easy his poetry flows:

'*Vom Eise befreit sind Strom und Bäche / von des Frühlings holden, belebenden Blick* . . . Or, in your language:

'"Released from ice are brook and river / by the quickening glance of the gracious spring . . ."' she recited, in her heavily accented English, before expounding why the literary world accorded the German poet, dramatist and philosopher equal place with Shakespeare and Dante.

This was my cue.

'Ah, Dante,' I cried. And not wanting to be outdone in literary appreciation, I quoted the first lines from the *Inferno* in my best Italian, as drawn from the memory recesses of my third-year studies, which immediately endeared me to the signora.

Paolo's grandfather was a mild-mannered, soft-spoken

man who hid his astute business acumen under an old-world charm. He made no secret of his obsession with family tradition.

When I first met him, Signor Minetti had eyed me coolly, assessing my position in Paolo's life, and barely hiding his disapproval when I moved in with his grandson. It was apparent that he did not even accept mitigating circumstances for my change of residence: the fact that the building in the Santa Croce district, in which I was renting a furnished room in a students' flat, had to be evacuated due to a gas explosion on a lower floor and the ensuing threat of structural collapse – a none-too-rare occurrence in the city's old quarter.

But then I was a *straniera* – a foreigner – and a non-catholic, disadvantages which, as a word here and there suggested, would disqualify me a priori as a potential wife. However, faced with a *fait accompli*, he was wise enough not to alienate Paolo, or endanger their working relationship, by ringing bells of displeasure in his ears. Instead, applying diplomacy worthy of a Lampedusa prince, he outwardly accepted me, while I was in no doubt that despite our literary rapport, his wife entertained the hope that her grandson would soon tire of *la inglesa*, pretty and educated though she was, and bring home a nice Italian signorina, preferably of Florentine extraction.

Over the weeks Signor Minetti's attitude towards me mellowed perceptibly. It seemed to suggest that my obvious lack of morals did not have any adverse effect on his grandson. The young man was never late for work, nor fell asleep over some intricate piece of craft. On the contrary, he continued to cultivate his business sense, and he was always smartly turned out in the show-room. Besides, whenever Signor Minetti called unexpectedly at his grandson's flat it was never offensively untidy and bore no resemblance to a den of licentiousness. Also, to all intents and purposes, Paolo's health did not seem to suffer from cohabiting with me. And how, so a warm smile finally betrayed one day, could a young foreign lady, who was able to converse in drawing-room Italian, and expatiate on the merits of the Quattro- and Quintocento with some eloquence, not grow on him, especially since she observed all the niceties of Italian social etiquette?

8

The rain was bucketing down when I went out. I wore rubber boots, and a voluminous raincoat which I had discovered among the effects of the late Signora Rossi, Paolo's mother. The young Claire would have preferred to get her jeans-clad thighs drenched, rather than walk about in a tent-like oilskin. However, the older woman in me held her physical comfort dear, and I thus saw no reason to risk a cold in what would shortly become a thoroughly unwholesome place.

I had all day to play the visionary, all day for what I saw as a hopeless, but morally compulsive task. The Claire I knew best had come to the fore, and just as she would normally plan a lecture, structure a paragraph or organise her household duties, she now set about selling her sinister news: And she was quite prepared to suffer the fate of door-to-door double-glazing salesmen, or Jehovah's Witnesses, who more often than not have the door slammed into their faces. Yes, Claire was back at the helm – at least until the light would fade and Paolo inevitably draw me back into his sorcerer's realm.

The city presented a picture of unrelieved grey that morning. Streaming wet, heaving with noisy traffic, umbrellas and sour-faced pedestrians, the stark contrast between its street life and its treasures enshrined in museums, churches and cloisters had never struck me quite so powerfully before. The thought that this gulf would have narrowed, once an undiscerning current was invading the city, befouling, defacing, warping and desecrating, put urgency into my steps.

I first went to the Palazzo Vecchio, hoping that the city fathers in their time-honoured vision might give credence to my warning and, at the risk of appearing over-cautious, take the necessary measures, to save many of the city's treasures, prevent loss of life and reduce suffering.

An office-to-office search produced no one of rank or authority. 'There's a national holiday tomorrow,' a clerk told me. 'The annual Armed Forces Day, that's why the city is beflagged. Some councillors are preparing for it, others have taken off for the weekend. Anyway, the local met office has issued no warning. So please go home, signorina. We have no time for worriers or forecasters of doom.'

The Biblioteka Nazionale was next on my list.

'The flood will destroy over a million books and ancient manuscripts,' I wailed at the grey-haired librarian. But he looked at me with the tolerance of his age and half a century of experience, in which days of persistent rain – while raising the level of the Arno – had brought the people of Florence no greater distress than wet feet.

As I left, my mission failed, I could not refrain from breathing at this august keeper of the written word, 'Don't say I didn't warn you!'

I looked at my watch. There was still time to go to the Choistro Verde before it closed for lunch. My legs, aware of the custodian's sacred siesta hour, accelerated.

Except for labouring traffic at its Loggia end, the Piazza Santa Maria Novella was deserted. So was the forecourt of the church, where – save for a few greedy siblings – the pigeons were sheltering from the heavy rain under the blind, arched windows of the church. At the nearby kiosk, where the vendor held a mere peephole open for prospective customers, while his wire racks, normally clasping newspapers, and assortments of picture postcards ranging from pink Florentine sunsets, churches, famous statues and master paintings to maxi-sized close-ups of David's genitalia, were covered with plastic sheeting.

As I stepped down to the cloister, I was seized by a strong sense of purpose. But I wasn't kidding myself. I knew full well that my motive was not entirely unselfish.

The custodian recognised me immediately.

'What, you again, signorina?'

'This time I have come on urgent business,' I said. 'I must speak to the Prior or to one of the Fathers.'

The young man scratched his head.

'I don't know . . . the Fathers are preparing for a special Mass, and the Prior never sees visitors without an appointment.'

Just then a priest in his soutane passed unhurriedly through a door into the colonnade, a Bible under his arm, his eyes fixed to the ground.

I rushed forward.

'*Scusi*, padre, could I please speak to you? It's terribly urgent.'

'*Si?*' The priest paused in his track.

The words clotted in my mouth as I watched his pious expression shifting to one of worldy irritation at being short-circuited in his inner communion by a young woman of positively northern looks and with a foreign accent. Behind him, in the background under the dusky vaulted ceiling, the disturbing lunette of Ucello's fresco mocked me with its dissolved contours and enfeebled colours.

'Father,' I began.

But my warning fell on deaf ears, as did my advice to barricade the entrance to the Piazza with sandbags. Perhaps, I thought, the preaching of the Roman Catholic Church still upheld the medieval belief that only witches and the devil's own disciples claimed the unholy gift of precognition, and that in this day and age, the enlightened sixties, none but the weather forecasters and their sensitive instruments were able to predict natural disasters. That, on the other hand, one was prudently keeping an open mind as to the competence of visionaries approved by the Church.

The priest's eyes narrowed. Let's stick to the prophets in Holy Scripture, his mien suggested, and his reply was studied, safe and tested.

'My dear child, I'm sure you're worrying unduly. There are no indications . . . Perhaps a prayer . . . There's much power in prayer to calm an anxious mind.'

'But Ucello's fresco, and the frescoes in the Spanish Chapel,' I cried, anger in my voice. 'Don't you understand, Father, the water will rise ten feet and more. It will leave so much destruction . . . '

But the priest had already turned his back to me. And there was now haste in his stride, as if *il diavolo* himself had thrown a female clairvoyant between his legs like a temptation of the flesh.

At the Uffici it proved as impossible to gain access to the curator's office as it would to steal a world-catalogued painting. I finally got hold of a pallid underling dressed like an undertaker, who badly disguised his annoyance at being confronted by a water-dripping foreigner. Frantic by now, I delivered my piece about the river going to breach the parapets and flood the best part of the city in the early hours of the morning.

'*Our* picture galleries are on the *upper* floors,' the young man informed me, offensive in his insinuation that I had never set foot in this illustrious building, and firmly leading me back to the door.

'But the restoration rooms are in the *basement*,' I retorted, being in no mood to suffer this fool lightly. 'I know, for a fact that among other paintings you have several Biccis, Lorenzos and Nicolòs down there at the moment, also the Velasquez self-portrait, some frescoes, tapestries—'

'Signorina,' the young man cut in. 'I'm sure—'

'The water will reach the ceiling in the basement,' I continued, unwavering. 'Will you please let someone in authority know. I'm no freak, and I'm in full possession of my faculties.'

The bland face nodded an easy assent. '*Bene, bene,* signorina.'

As the door closed behind me, I knew that he had not believed a single word.

Undisturbed by wandering tourists, in the unremitting rain, the quadrangle leading to the Piazzi Chapel and the Sante Croce Museum effused a bleak serenity. I passed the Corinthian columns of the porticoed chapel and, unnoticed by the attendant, slipped into an adjoining, much smaller inner courtyard, where grilled cell windows, heavily shaded by a colonnade, overlooked a sodden lawn. I strolled around, professing an interest in arches, pilasters and cornices, until I spied a monk's garb through a door left ajar.

'*Scusi*,' I called, making desperate signs of urgency.

The friar widened the gap of the door by several inches and stared, wide-eyed, at the female trespasser in her outsized raincoat.

'Please, listen to me,' I began, 'and I swear to God that I'm not making this up: the city will be hit by a terrible flood early tomorrow morning. I know that the church, the chapel and the refectory will be inundated by up to twenty feet of oily water. It will deface and flake colour off frescos, damage panels and sculptures. Cimabue's Crucifix will be the greatest loss. The grimy water will eat into the figure of Christ and destroy seventy per cent of the surface. The whole art world will be crying over it. And you and the Brothers and voluntary helpers will be wading in water and muck for days, sieving it for fragments of paints. Perhaps sandbags ... or could you try and move the Cross to a safer place?'

I leaned against the wall. Tears welled up behind my eyes, blinding me, but I was not sure whether in frustration over my failure to ring alarm bells in the genial-looking friar, or because I was already grieving for Cimabue's ravaged thirteenth-century masterpiece, widely considered to be the most poignant relic of the Christian world.

The monk's voice was paternal, patient, propitiatory:

'My dear young lady, this dreadful rain ... it is bound to make any of us fear the worst. But the river has often swollen dangerously in the past, without causing a flood. I'm sure you're assuming the worst. However, it was good of you to come and voice your concern ... your anxiety.'

Another door closed.

I was tired and hungry. Despite my effective rain gear I felt the dampness creeping under my clothes and into my boots. A hot coffee and a *panino proscuetto* revived my spirits and sped me on to my next port of call: the Public Record Office, where I knew scores of ancient documents would be damaged or destroyed by water, mud and oil. But here, as in other churches, museums and archives which – so I remembered from photographic evidence and media accounts at the time – had taken the brunt of the flood, my warning elicited only indulgent smiles or, at best, the assurance that the authorities were bound to keep an eye on the situation.

Dusk fell early that afternoon. I counted the hours, before the river Arno would take the city by surprise. The shock of realizing how little time was left instantly dispatched me on another errand. Once again, I felt like a scientist trying to modify a law of nature. You're mad, I told myself – history allows neither moron nor genius to make even a minor correction. But an irrational sense of responsibility drove me on.

This time my targets were the antiquarians grouped in the Via dei Fossi and Via Moro, who were known to store an arsenal of priceless furniture, paintings, tapestries and *objets d'art* in their street-level storerooms and basements, and who – I realised with a mental shudder – would be hardest hit among the city's shop-keepers. In my mind's eye I saw their irreplaceable goods being sluiced from their shops by raging waters, carried like flotsam through the streets, and finally left stuck in the mud – the victims of nature's ravages.

By now agitated like a traveller who fears to miss the last train or flight, I negotiated a rapid-swollen gutter and turned into the network of alleys. If only one antiquarian would heed my warning, I thought, thus saving a few items from their ignominious death, then this last leg of my mission would not have been wasted.

However, as expected, I earned myself nothing but polite snubs or patronising smiles, before an assistant would resolutely usher me out. In one shop, helped by mirrors during my voluntary retreat, I espied a dealer shooting a meaningful glance at his assistant, while tapping his temple with his forefinger.

Some were more outspoken. Trade, they said, was not at

its best at this time of the year, particularly in pouring rain. So they needed foreigners, mocking them with wild stories about an impending deluge, like they needed a hole in the head.

At last I stood on the Ponte Vecchio, feet aching, wet strands of hair dangling from under my hood like aquatic weeds.

The Minetti shop. A patrician brass-enhanced door, the kind which could have claimed pride of place in mediaeval Chichester or Stratford-upon-Avon. A shop window set into a polished wood surround, displaying a scintillating assortment of jewellery, gold and silver ware. A shop whose frontage effused tradition, the quality of goods and an age-old honoured trade.

I weighed my chances of success. Should I, in one last attempt at depriving the river of some of its booty, confront Paolo's grandfather, risking an open rebuff from Paolo, and being treated by the old man – if not with the forbearance of his age – like someone suffering from a particularly virulent strain of pessimism?

A chatty English couple entering the shop relieved me of a decision, and I slogged back through the rain to what was likely to be my home for an indefinite period. I saw myself as an ant which had tried all day to move a rock. But there was no time for dejection. Time was precious, and I still had to take care of a few chores, one of which, top on my list, was to fill the bath and every container with water before midnight. 'Be prepared!' The motto ingrained in the young Claire's approach to life had always stood me in good stead, and I suddenly realised that it might never find a more pertinent application.

At the thought of sharing Paolo's bed again that night, of caressing the perfection of his body, like Michelangelo might have run self-congratulatory fingers over his chiselled image of masculine beauty and virility, I felt a sweetness stirring in my blood – an exquisite budding and burgeoning of desire, whiched seemed to make the approaching catastrophe peripheral.

9

I woke in the middle of the night, the memory of our love-making still luxuriating on every inch of my skin and between my thighs; the memory of Paolo's splendid nudity, of my own pounding, joyous spasms . . . ebbing away into a boundless tenderness.

The rain was hitting the flat roof above like a sonorous roll of drums, while slashing against the shutters. Down below, scarcely audible through the din, there broke the sound of car tyres skating over wet cobblestones.

I felt warm and safe, shielded from nature's agony by Paolo's arm and the rhythmic rise and fall of his breathing close to my ear. Hard as I tried, I did not find my way back to sleep. As the minutes ticked by like a hypnotist's swinging pendulum, my mind became prey to the solitude of wakefulness, prey to the proliferation and distortion of thoughts, and – now and again – to soaring flashes of clear-sightedness and robust reasoning. It raced forward to the future, to my former time, to Charles.

My inner eye rested in my London bedroom, where Charles was ensconced in bed behind Pascal, Rochefoucauld or Rousseau, having first wished me 'Good night' and brushed my lips in a muted declaration of love which, in my interpretation, doubled up as an apology for preferring the pleasures of an erudite book to those of the carnal kind – Saturday nights excepted.

And yet: Charles and I were ideal partners. We spoke the same language, we had a similar background. We both loved Bach, Mozart and opera; cathedrals, old trees and things old-wordly. We loved vintage wines and home-cooked fare, hot summers, lone stretches of languid rivers, country lanes, bird song, roses, tradition and the company of friends, not to speak of such modest delights as the smell of cut grass, freshly-ground coffee and oven-warm bread. And, of course, we both loved books, described by greater minds than ours as 'ambrosia for the mind'.

Politically, too, we had the same leanings – an advantage, cynics claim, which keeps peace in the living-room. Indeed, we enjoy more common ground. We like to discuss abstract ideas, and at times we even venture on to esoteric ground; while, spiritually, we are both untiring in our quest for answers in the grand scheme of things.

And what is more: we never developed a fixation on each other's negative traits, or the odd irritating habit, which so often reverses the magic process of being in love, by sowing the seeds of alienation. Instead, we always had the courage directly to confront each other and negotiate peacefully whatever was nagging our mental Achilles' heels. It worked. By remaining open and flexible in our approach to each other, we have so far always sailed triumphantly through every marital hiccup that might have weakened our relationship. Perhaps over the years, such affinity of spirit and ease of partnership has gradually tamed our love-making – into pre-programmed sexual outings like congenial rambles in a picturesque but flat countryside . . .

A sudden toss and turn of the body beside me terminated my mental meanderings and firmly put thoughts of Charles behind bars. I thought the rain had eased off a little, and instead of beating the roof like a military bandsman a bass drum it now produced gentler sounds – like children rapping their knuckles on the stretched parchment of toy drums, which, shaken as a housewife sieves flour, made their little bells jingle.

By then I was fathoms back into sleep.

It must have been well after midnight when the dogs started barking and howling in the neighbourhood, and Sarah scratched at the bedroom door, issuing pathetic miaows. The racket startled but did not surprise me. For I realised that in a count-down to zero hour, the animals' acute senses were warning them of an approaching cataclysm of nature, just as the creatures of the earth, through some higher instinct, might have divined the biblical deluge. Calmly, I wondered whether at this moment the birds of Tuscany were twittering away excitedly in the darkness, and caged birds were fluttering about their cages with the impotence of prisoners. Perhaps farm animals were equally restless in stables, pens and byres, causing sleep-heavy farmers to leave their beds and check outside for trouble.

And the small creatures in the field?

Would instinct draw them from their dens and burrows, to dance fretfully about, or make them move to higher ground, being plagued by occult vibrations which man's most sophisticated instruments could not pick up?

The telephone rang. Paolo grunted himself awake and groped for the receiver.

'Si, si, I'll come as fast as I can,' he said, and shot out of bed. For seconds he stood as naked and lost as Adam after God had confronted him with his sudden existence.

'That was my grandfather,' Paolo explained. 'He's had a telephone call from Romildo Cesaroni, the private watchman on the Ponte Vecchio. He says he's never seen the river rising like this before. So he's warning all the jewellers and goldsmiths with shops on the bridge.'

'Your grandfather obviously believes him.'

'Well, he thinks Romildo might have exaggerated. Might have been over-cautious in raising the alarm. But he feels it would be prudent to go and check for ourselves. If necessary, he says, we can clear out our most valuable stock.'

With some difficulty I refrained from pointing out that this was what I had been urging them to do.

'It may, of course, come to nothing,' Paolo added, 'but then we will have lost no more than an hour's sleep.'

'I'm glad your grandfather doesn't ignore the watchman's warning,' I said. 'Other jewellers will. They'll doubt his assessment of the river's behaviour. They'll argue that it has often reached a high level in the past, without flooding the city. And they'll just turn over in bed.'

'Here you go again, darling,' said Paolo, as if scolding some young miscreant.

But I had not finished yet, not by a long way.

'You'd better hurry,' I urged, 'the river will breach its banks shortly after three.'

'For heaven's sake, Claire!'

'Can I help you with anything?'

'I'll need a large suitcase.'

'And a torch.'

'What on earth for?'

'The electricity will go.'

Paolo stayed silent. He wrenched himself into a pair of denims and struggled into a pullover, the arms of which were turned inside out. My mind flashed across the abyss of Time. Paul, I thought. This could have been my son – the teenager, forever undressing at bedtime with the negligence and haste of his age, leaving his jeans in a crumpled heap, his underpants as a sausage-like piece of fabric, his socks lone nests of cotton and polyester;

the frustrated dresser battling with disobliging trousers, tops and footwear, minutes before the school bus was due, and – books under one arm – downing a glass of orange juice, before gusting out of the house with a cheery 'Bye, Mum; bye, Dad!' And I hate to think what his clothes-shedding routine is like in his student digs . . . .

The mother in me was aching, but Claire's new reality soon claimed my attention.

Paolo was about to slip on his shoes, when I produced a pair of rubber boots from a closet.

'Here, wear these.'

'What's this?'

'I bought them yesterday. You'll need them.'

Paolo's face turned into a still life of questions and confusion. 'Christ, Claire, you're dead serious, aren't you? Is that why you filled the bath last night, and why you bought all those tins? I'm afraid I came across them by accident, while I was looking for something. What on earth . . . surely we're not in for a famine.'

'No, but for a terrible disaster,' I said a trifle tartly and went in search of a suitcase.

At the door, holding an umbrella in one hand and a suitcase in the other, Paolo smiled one of his glorious smiles at me.

'Keep my side of the bed warm, chiara, I'll be back soon.'

I watched him swiftly descending the stairs in the dim stairway light. Back in the flat, I went to the window. A car door slammed, tyres screeched. Through a curtain of rain I watched headlights shooting out of sight. I shivered, as my skin reacted to sudden quivers of foreboding in the air. Pulling Paolo's bathrobe tightly around me, I went into the kitchen and filled a Thermos flask with hot coffee, another with boiling water. A cup of steaming tea finally returned me to warmth and sleepiness.

In bed, the young Claire burrowed her head into Paolo's pillow and slung an arm over his side of the duvet, while the older woman listened resignedly to the sputter of rain and for charted events to take their course.

When I opened my eyes again an eerie stillness floated into the room through the patter of rain and the grey light of dawn. A singular thought exploded in my head: The flood. O God, the flood! The streets would be awash by now, and this would account for the absence of familiar morning sounds: motorcars starting up or needling their way through the narrow street, Vespas trying to match in decibels the horse-power of heavy motorcycles, doors opening and closing, or slamming on garrulous dialogues behind those off to work. But then, today was a national holiday, and most Florentines would want to lie in. Anyway, where were they to go, now that the streets were bound to be non-navigable canals?

Copious, three-dimensional images of the devastation under way plastered my mind: Basement dwellers waking up in their beds as on sinking islands; stinking water, carrying oil and sewage and the contents of a thousands rubbish bins, reigning supreme as marauder, vandal, polluter and king of the streets.

But such nightmarish pictures now no more than pinpricked me with their messages. For I felt drained of the power and pain of foreknowledge, sad, rather than frustrated, at my failure to make people take note of my warning and save at least a fraction from damage and destruction of what – looked at with hindsight, and with a nod to the unshakability of the past – was fated to be damaged or destroyed. Resigned to a mere spectator's role for a day or two, I prepared myself to watch nature's aggression from under a pain-proofed umbrella of sentiments.

I reached out, groped for physical contact with Paolo,

with a fellow-being. But his side of the bed was empty, cold from the absence of hours. At the foot of the bed, well out of my reach, Sarah lay curled up, sleeping.

'Paolo!' I cried. And louder, 'Paolo!' But only silence echoed through the half-open bedroom door. The cat woke up, stretched, yawned and arched her back as if it were made of rubber. Having narrowly glanced at me, she jumped and walked away.

I was assailed by a violent sense of isolation. Yet an explanation was at hand. Paolo might have taken his grandfather and their stock back to the Via Ricasoli. And, not realising that behind him the river had burst its banks, he might have procrastinated. Perhaps a hot drink, the drying of wet clothes, speculations as to the river containing itself, as it had done so many times, or mutual congratulations on having carried out a successful pre-dawn rescue. Finally, on finding the insurging waters cutting his way off, Paolo would have had no alternative but to remain where he was, housebound in the Via Ricasoli.

Without much enthusiasm I viewed the prospect of spending the next few days islanded with Sarah and a mountain of tinned food, while the thought of being walled-in with my other self was decidedly unattractive.

I got out of bed and went to the window. Without haste. For I knew what I would find below. However, when I opened the shutters, reality far exceeded my expectations and instilled an acute sense of emergency.

A yellowish-brown mass of water, already several feet deep, was churning through the street. Seen from above, it formed abstract flow patterns – spiralling whirlpools, bubbling spots, where collapsed drains were regurgitating effluent, counter-flow drifts caused by swirling turbulence encountering obstacles.

Detritus was bobbing past: branches still in leaf, motorcars, timber, an oil drum, a tailor's dummy, petrol cans, a doll, an upturned bow-legged chair. I mused: What a grand obnoxious show, watched over by a morbid sky.

The fetid current conducted its own orchestra, as it hurled objects against walls, jumped hurdles or bypassed obstructions – sounds swishing, metallic, jarring or grating, yet not clamorous enough to stand out against the plodding rain and jerk sleepers from their beds.

I flicked the light switch. Nothing. The electricity had gone. The phone? Here was my chance to communicate with Paolo. But it was dead. In the kitchen, the last water oozed from the taps, and I applauded myself on my forethought in turning the bath into a water trough. And now the Girl Guide in me worked to a list of priorities.

I had a cup of coffee from the flask, washed – if somewhat sketchily – and slipped on one of Paolo's warmest pullovers. After a frugal breakfast I put candles around the rooms, surveyed my provisions and fed the cat. Only then did I return to the window and watch the water rising. But now shutters were opened opposite and below me, and heads strained towards the deluge below. Cries of shock, excitement or plain anguish were spinning crisscross patterns between the buildings.

I went downstairs in the vain hope that it might not be too late to help Signor Ribaldi, the fine-leather craftsman, to evacuate his botthega. But it was completely awash.

An agitated group of residents had gathered on the first-floor landing.

'Poor Signor Ribaldi,' they cried, 'he's visiting his sister's family over the weekend, and no one has the key to his shop.' Not that it would do any good, they added, now that the basement and most of the shop were under water. Cursing *il fiume maledetto*, the damned river, they stared at the filthy water creeping up the stairs inch by inch as if hypnotised by the river's malevolence. They cried, 'Santa Maria,' appealed to the Saints, and crossed themselves.

One man, cynicism in his voice, saw the flood as a harbinger of The Last Judgement, what with mankind, and modern corrupt and greedy society in particular. Another man, eager to show off his use of analogy, likened the happening to the Biblical Deluge.

'This is how it must have started then. As the Good Book says, "And all the windows of heaven opened and the flood was upon the earth . . . "'

'Oh, stop it,' wailed a woman. 'You're a proper prophet of doom. The water will go down again. I remember, in nineteen hundred and . . . '

But no one listened.

Once they had regained their breath and a modicum of equilibrium, they responded with measured politeness to my offer of assistance should the water threaten to reach the first floor flats.

'Gracie, signorina,' they said, but their vote of thanks did not deceive me. For even months after the young Claire had come to share Paolo's flat, their eyes still mirrored disapproval of *la inglesa* who was cohabiting with such a fine chap as Signor Minetti without the 'blessings of the church'.

'*Dove é il signor?*' they asked.

I told them about the watchman's warning and verbalised my suspicion that the breach of the Arno, and the waters flooding into the heart of the city, had taken Paolo by surprise. And what bad luck that the phones were dead and we would now have to sit out the flood in separate apartments.

Back upstairs, there came the dull sound of explosions, and I knew that heating boilers in basements all over the city were blowing up, injecting yet more black, sticky oil into the milling current, which would rise to the surface, to form helical patterns and evil-looking drifts.

I switched on Paolo's transistor radio.

An Italian voice, weak, oscillating, punctuated by static interference. A fractured newsline:

'... the situation in Florence is growing more and more dramatic... Arno continues to rise... never before recorded in the history of the city...'

I turned up the volume, extended the aerial, tuned my way through nebulous wave bands, until I located a BBC voice. Barely audible, his vowels fluctuating on the near-terminal battery power of the small set, the newscaster informed his listeners that two million Red Guards were parading in Peking. Then came a sound as of someone walking over potato crisps, before the set blared forth nothing but silence. The batteries were dead. My communion with the world on dry land had ceased.

Buried in the depths of an armchair, Paolo's pullover covering my thighs like a rug, I opened a century-old family Bible. What better time, I thought, to read up the chapter on the Deluge and, in the midst of a real twentieth-century cataclysm, compare it with Ucello's vision of 'Il Diluvio'.

'... and the windows of heaven were opened. And the rain was upon the earth...'

In the spirit of the hour, which tolerated no enmity between man and beast, I called over to Sarah, who had taken up her seat on the window seat again, perhaps the better to watch the drama unfolding below or, from the corner of her eye, to watch me.

'Cat,' I said, 'we're in a fine mess. And since it looks as if it'll be only you and me for the next day or two, and you'd be feeling awfully lonely, keeping your distance the way you do, why not come over for a bit of companionship?'

The cat looked at me as if rating the sincerity of my offer. Then, in a fitting change of mood, yet without undue haste, she jumped to the floor, strode majestically to within a foot of me and sat down. With her tail coiled around her, her head erect as if crowned, and her green eyes unblinking, she looked a picture of feline grace. I patted my lap.

The cat jumped.

Thus I sat in my upholstered ark, waiting for the waters to abate from the streets, and feeling safe from the fury nature had unleashed upon Florence and its citizens. As I read on, penetrating, chapter by chapter, into a territory into which I had not mentally set foot since Sunday-School days, my two-level cogitations, concerns and conjectures, fell off me. And now I was no more than a human being who in times of disaster takes refuge in the Bible and keeps close to anything that breathes and is warm-blooded and friendly.

Soon Sarah's contented purring and her body heat generated in me a sense of comfort and drowsiness, which preyed on my reading attention and lulled me into an unaccustomed mid-morning sleep.

Towards midday a heavy thud brought me to the window. An uprooted tree, swept into the roaring canyon below, had struck the house wall opposite like a battering ram and come to rest so awkwardly between buildings that its snarling roots impeded the flow of water, thus forming new troughs, swills and secondary currents. Having risen by several feet, and still rising, the water now reeked of gas released from drains which – common knowledge to Florentines – had been laid when Tuscany was still a Duchy. Meanwhile, a multitude of sounds orchestrated the infernal show in the city's streets: wailing sirens from beyond the boundaries of inundation, motor-cars blaring their horns as water closed their electric circuits, helicopters droning overhead. And judging by intermittent plonking noises still more boilers were exploding in flooded districts.

The rain had thinned out, and there were now few

windows at which someone did not stand vigil, transmitting anxieties to neighbours across the street and to floors above or below. And it was not long before information was being passed on, bush-telegraph style, on the extent of the flood and the state of rescue operations:

'The Ponte Vecchio is almost completely under water – In the Santa Croce district people are stranded on rooftops – In the Via Tornabuoni, Dio mio, all the elegant shops are flooded – The Piazza del Duomo is a swirling lake – In the Gavinana quarter invalids have drowned in their beds . . . '

A woman wailed:

We have no water!'

A man's reassuring voice:

'Won't be long now, before they'll send in the army with their amphibian vehicles.'

Below, a yellow ball was bobbing past, pursued by wreckage. I closed the window against the offensive stench and buried my nose into the redolent hyacinth.

Shortly afterwards the rain stopped.

10

That night sleep refused to come. Too horrific had been the day's events, to block them off in my mind, too keenly was I reacting to nocturnal images of being immured for the duration of the flood. I tossed and turned. Progressively, the empty space beside me assumed a taunting, palpable presence. Both women were back: my rampant sexual self, and the young Claire. But as the latter embraced Paolo's pillow, the older woman listened to the seductive tango rhythms in her blood. My pelvis, my legs strained to get on to the dance floor. But I had no one to dance with.

By the light of a candle I finally took flight in a highly technical manual on the craft of silver bijouterie. Sleep, however, when it deigned to come, was neither of the recuperative nor of the drugged kind. Teasing, pleasing, torturing, it packed me off on a conducted tour through familiar premises . . .

Weightless, I transcend time barriers, back to the life in which I feel at home, just as if my dream, acting philosopher and disciplinarian, wants to impress upon me where my loyalties lie and, ultimately, my real happiness.

A garden manifests itself, my beloved oasis, my weekend Shangri–la, into which, season after season, I had poured my green passions. Sequestered behind stone walls and creepers, distanced from London traffic and, at the height of a fine English summer, holding the lusciousness and intimacy of a Tuscan garden, it is but short of a topiaried hedge, a weathered stone seat, oleander trees and the heat-vibrating air of southern climes. Smiling, I wander among terracotta urns of geraniums and dwarf conifers; I fill my lungs with the scents of box, clematis and wisteria; I pull a weed here and there, water rose beds and pick bright flashes of long-stemmed perennials.

Gently, my dreams eases me through the open patio doors into the drawing-room, where Charles is reading in his favourite chair, a drink by his side, the pipe in his mouth moving imperceptibly to the rhythm of the written word. A *soupçon* of a smile on his lips adds to the picture of physical and intellectual contentment.

'Charles,' I call out, but my husband of twenty years does not look up. My mind strains towards him, but my leg muscles do not obey its command. 'Look at me!' I cry, and, begging, 'Please, look at me!' But my voice is like gossamer, a filmy, floating substance that carries no sound.

A pluck at my sleeve intimates that it is time to move on. At this moment Charles raises his eyes and gazes at me – or, better, through me, as if he were listening to a blissful orchestral passage or the jubilation of a nightingale.

I feel an overpowering longing to touch and tell him that I am sorry I have gone away. And I would like to reassure him that I will try anything to plod my way back. That I shall be back. Sometime. If Time will let me.

The pull on my reins grows more insistent.

'Please, let me stay a little longer,' I plead with my dream-pilot, like a child clamouring for an extension of bed-time and testing parental power, like a teenager wanting to watch pop television instead of concentrating on his homework, and gauging his own rebellious breadth against his elders.

My guide was adamant.

'I'm afraid there's no time.'

'But I want to stay,' I cry out, short of stamping my foot. 'This is my home, and here, so close and yet so distant, is my husband whom I love dearly. And Paul, my son, will be home next weekend . . . '

'No antics, please,' said the voice with a strong censorious overtone. 'You have only yourself to blame, lady. You were perfectly aware of your blessings. Stirring the cauldron of the past, for whatever reasons, is asking for trouble.'

'But how can I get back?'

'Ah, there lies the rub,' said my partner in dialogue. 'I'm afraid this is up to the Court of Metaphysical Affairs. They might, of course, take the view that anyone who allows her mind to pursue adulterous practices, and her riotous imagination to gallop away with her, courts disaster and has a price to pay.

'What then will shift me back into my own time?' I asked. 'Ucello's fresco?'

'You will know when the time comes, I'm sure. The expiation of sins . . . '

The Winds of Time and Dimensions blasted the rest of the sentence away, as my pilot whisked me back through twenty years of vivid images which, lined by the wayside like billboards, epitomized all I was holding dear or had once treasured.

A dull ache established itself in my chest – the combined weight of frustration, self-pity and love drifting impotently in space . . .

I opened my eyes to a shaft of light invading the room through a chink of the curtain, and I remembered that

I had forgotten to close the shutters before going to bed. As I traced the pattern of light and shade on the ceiling, I was conscious of a luxuriant feeling of tranquillity that had my blood running cool and sober in my veins. I pondered briefly about the night's dream, before ditching it like impedimenta in view of the very realistic problems and tasks lying ahead, which required very down-to-earth efforts.

Once again the scary silence creeping up from the street quickly activated my brain cells, and I identified and itemized priorities as if I were making up a shopping list or enumerating points of artistic interest to a class of students. The Claire of wifely, motherly and scholarly status was back in control, even if the absence of lines on my face and the timid curve of my hips, impassively checked in the mirror, did not match the maturity of my thinking.

I opened the window wide to a pale blue sky and a pink sun rising over the cupola of the duomo. Down below, the water had receded, leaving behind tons of oil-daubed muck clotted with debris. At the off-side of the uprooted tree which had blocked the passage of larger pieces of wreckage, battered motor-cars formed a towering scrapheat camouflaged by a tangle of branches. Protruding from this monstrosity was a slat of timber firmly anchored between metal rods. At its feet, a perambulator reduced to a mangled chassis and rags stuck obscenely out of the knee-high mud.

'And the waters abated from the earth . . . ' so it echoed in my mind.

I quickly shut the window again, to keep out the infernal stench which was rising as lustily as wood smoke on a fine summer day, thus forming an invisible barrier against the Dantesque legacy of a river in spate, over which the rising sun, as the first witness, seemed to exclaim:

'O povera Firenze!'

Poor Florence, indeed. And now, with the story from Genesis never far from my mind, I wondered what the smell of the land must have been like, when the waters around the ark had gone down, and the chosen survivors of the deluge stepped through their hatches and greedily on to firm soil. Had a putrid, cadaverous odour affronted them, thinned, now and then, by a whiff of distant sea or alpine air, or had the land freed from the waters greeted them with the damp, verdant breath of lichen, moss, wet grasses and steaming autumnal soil? Or had there prevailed a salty, tangy odour, of seaweed and shell-encrusted rock and roots, sun-withered crustaceans and sprouting plant life?

I buried my nose into the hyacinth, stored its bouquet in my nostrils and declared an end to my musings. There was much work to be done.

At a time when English matrons meet for elevenses, and a cup of tea or coffee makes for office rituals, I put on my gum boots, knotted a red-and white headscarf under my chin and joined the first Florentines venturing into the streets.

Dismayed shop-keepers and basement dwellers armed with shovels, brooms and buckets, stared at a cleaning-up job which held out little hope for a speedy execution. The odd sightseer, and those trying to return home from wherever they had spent the last two nights, bravely stalked through the heavy scum as on stilts, eyes fixed on their dubious footings. Slipping and cursing, many were forced back by the sheer mass of mire. Some people wore rubber boots, some fishermen's waders; others, not so lucky, had fastened plastic bags around their shoes with string. Cries went out for food, water and medicines. Angry voices:

'When is the army coming? Hasn't Rome heard of our plight?'

A helicopter swept over the roof. From beyond the inundated districts, where roads were passable, the sound of sirens prevailed, feebly, not growing in volume, yet adding their own sinister note to the drama around. From under spewed-up cobblestones, from burst sewage pipes and the carcases of dogs – from scuttling rats and basement tombs – there rose the danger of an epidemic.

I heaved my legs past furniture sluiced out of an antique shop and gingerly stepped over ledgers and cardboard boxes reduced to a pulp. I trod on items unrecognisable under their tarnish or buried in thick slime. I was saddened by the sight of a florist's former splendour poking out of its boggy grave – a caked mess of mangled flower heads, bare stems and foliage stained the colour of tar. I plodded through the stinking quagmire as through the effluent of Hell. And not even the spectacle of a tailor's dummy, which had come to rest on the squashed boot of a car, its legs splayed suggestively, managed to arouse in me a flicker of humour.

The thought of Paolo labouring his way home through the befouled streets, and a decision fermenting in my mind like young wine, made me head back. I acquired a shovel from among the muddy remnants of an ironmonger's shop and joined the brigade of flood victims and volunteers. Shifting, shovelling and slopping out, I felt part of a fellowship of people who, regardless of political leanings and social disparity, had united in a common effort.

Since I was the only resident in the building with a camping stove and a supply of water, I made a bucketful of coffee and ladled it out among my toiling neighbours. As the clock moved on, I extended my services, by turning Paolo's *cocina* into a field-kitchen. I did so with a smile and an overflowing reservoir of energy. I heated tins of soup, cooked pasta and boiled water. And they came and queued with jugs and bowls, silently, as if humiliated by the generosity of the *straniera,* the 'floozy', at whom they used to look askance, granting her no more than a narrow greeting whenever they passed her on the stairway or in the street, and this most likely not so much in a miserly acknowledgement of my persona than out of respect for Signor Paolo, who was a Minetti. But the spirit of the hour tolerated no gritting teeth, no sheepish faces. As my smile loosened their uncomfortable expressions, and a war-time spirit spread among the tenants, Florentine witticism of the ironic or pungent kind added spice to the simple meal. For now it was time for comradeship, time also for a *'tante gracie*, signorina!' and a straight look into the eye.

But where was Paolo? Was the Via Riconsoli still blocked, unassailable even for a young man of athletic prowess? Had he perhaps sprained an ankle during his toilsome rescue trip? Or had the exertion, and the anxious moments on the Ponte Vecchio, been too much for the old man? Questions which were causing draughts like open doors, and giving access to the worms of disquietude.

When I had closed the door on the last of my neighbours that day, I pondered the miracle that had made the burner gas last, and the food and water go round. Perhaps, I thought, here was the stuff for a modern parable.

I felt great. In the strange design of things I had been given a role to play, which left me no time for introspective expeditions. I remembered my dream. I recalled British news coverage in the days and weeks following the flood. And now a path emerged from out of my hazy vision, logical, linear and lonely, one which disregarded the laws of perspective by having no vanishing point.

I knocked on a neighbour's door. *Si*, they had heard the news, no, there had been nothing on the radio about a state of emergency, no instructions to householders as to how to cope without food and water. Only a warning – how farcical! – that the water in and around Florence was heavily polluted.

The retired schoolmaster spat out his rage.

'The sheer incompetence of the authorities! No one gave us any warning.' And, on a lighter, befriending note, 'Will you stay, signorina, and have a glass of wine with us?'

That night, the walls out of reach of the timorous light of my bedside candle, threatened to close in on me. The empty bed space beside me eagerly sought answers. I thought of Florence cut off by rail, road and telephone, a city moaning under its muck and weeping at the sight of despoilation; I brooded over my isolation on a foreign time shore. My mind was spinning. But although every fibre of my body was aching for sleep, the blissful anaesthesia of the just evaded me.

I reached for Petrarca's verses, but their lyricism made my physical and emotional exile only more tangible. As a last resort – my pen is ashamed to record the tardiness of such thought – I opened the Bible again, the very book which throughout the centuries had prepared Christian eventide readers for Morpheus' arms. And it was not long now before there came over me a peace which, acting like mulled wine, cradled me into a dreamless sleep.

11

As soon as I saw Paolo's grandfather, I knew that something was terribly wrong.

There had always been an air of gentle assertiveness about Signor Minetti, a confidence of blood, social status, wealth and manners, which found an unwitting expression in the sexagenarian's bearing and the bright calm of his eyes. Yet that morning, as he opened the door, his shoulders were hunched, his eyes lustreless, and his lips quivered with the vain effort of attempting a smile. His voice alone should have warned me. It was flat and barely audible.

'Come in, Claire.'

'What a dreadful disaster!' I exclaimed. 'I just had to come and check whether you and Paolo and the *signora* are all right. It's been days . . . I've been getting worried. You have no idea what the city looks like. And the stench! In some places it is overpowering. This is what it must have been like in the days of open sewers.' At pains to sound like the young Claire, I added that the streets resembled an obstacle course designed for athletes and acrobats. But Signor Minetti failed to react to my informative chatter with even the hint of a smile.

In the 'big room' daylight squeezed through half-drawn curtains, light too frugal to expel the air of cold magnificence, too hesitant even vainly to mirror itself in the silver centre-pieces.

I rattled on about my hazardous trek; I wailed about the damage the flood had caused, and that it would be days before the whole extent of it would be known. Only then did I ask:

'Where is Paolo?'

The old man cleared his throat and pointed to a seat. His hands fidgeted, his lips thinned. Agony clouded his brow. Once again I was conscious of a chill wind of foreboding.

'My grandson . . . Paolo . . . is missing, presumed dead,' gasped Signor Minetti, visibly dwindling in his chair: 'They say the flood might have swept him off his feet and washed him down the river, and that he wouldn't have had a chance. If only he had listened to me and not gone back . . . '

'Oh, no,' I wailed, covering my face with my hands, as if to ward off the news. 'If only . . . ' Like the opening bars of a lament, the two words hung dark and anguished in the room. A few minutes later I had the full story. Of how, when they arrived, Paolo and his grandfather found the bridge trembling under the impact of the swollen Arno, whose waters were travelling at sixty kilometres per hour, its level still rising, while Carabineri shouted against the rumbling of the intoxicated river:

'You'll have to hurry, folks, no one can tell whether the bridge will hold!'

The drama unfolds. Having stuffed their choice objects and customers' articles into their suitcases, while the floor under their feet is shaking and urging haste, Paolo and his grandfather struggle back to the Lugarno, where a few late-night motorists have gathered. And here the story of the two men's rescue bid ought to end. But Paolo, fearless, confident, and acting against the older man's advice, decides to make another trip back to the shop, to retrieve items of business and sentimental value. By now, motor cars are beaming blazing headlights on to the bridge, stage-lighting the savage scene. All too visibly the situation is worsening steadily. In the pouring rain, and forced into a spectator's role, Signor Minelli refuses to be shifted until Carabineri are yelling:

'*Si salve che può!* The bridge may collapse any minute!'

There come the thudding, crashing sounds of tree trunks charging against the lower windows of the bridge and into showrooms like high-powered battering rams. A mighty roar, and the seething current billows and sweeps through the arches and breeches of the Ponte and out again on the other side, gutting shops. And now, not a minute too early, Carabineri marshal sightseers away from the Lungarno, cars are speeding off, lone pedestrians are taking to their heels. The first swell of water spills, then gushes over the embankment, soon to run amok through the city.

'I pleaded with Paolo,' moaned Signor Minetti. '"Don't go back," I said. "Don't take the risk." But I suppose, like most young men, he thought muscles and a bit of daring would be enough.'

I was seized by conflicting emotions. One part of me, reaching back to the spring and high summer of her love affair, grieved at what with increasing certainty appeared to be Paolo's death; my other self, her fitful desires already consigned to the past, her inner compass reset to a hopeful re-entry into her own time, sighed with relief.

But then any emotional tug-of-war makes a mess of one's equilibrium. I knew. That is, my older self knew. And it was she who now cut off the young Claire's lifeline. Her demise was clean, swift and painless. The young woman did not struggle, nor did she weep. She just faded away like a ghost which had at last found eternal peace.

'How is the signora taking it?' I asked.

'She's resting,' replied Signor Minelli who in a choking voice had been cursing the river which had claimed his grandson's life. 'Her heart . . . you know, she adored the boy.'

'Is there anything I can do for you and the signora? Are you all right for food and water? You won't be able to set foot in the streets for quite a few days.'

Signor Minelli assured me that, luckily, there were enough supplies to last them for a week.

'We even have powdered milk and candles,' he said. 'I had no idea that my wife had stocked up the larder for an emergency situation. She's a bit cagey about what made her do it . . . says she's had a dream which warned her of the flood, or something like it. Well, I'm not arguing with her, for we're obviously better off for it.'

A laboured smile flitted over the troubled face.

But now my thoughts were galloping ahead, blatantly realistic, practical. Paolo's flat. Did his death spell my eviction? If so, where was I to go?

'I'm sorry,' I said, 'this may not be the right time to bring up the matter, but I'm afraid I need to know what you intend to do with Paolo's flat. Will you be selling or letting it right away? If not, would you allow me to stay on there until I've found alternative accommodation, or until . . . I can go home . . . I mean, until I've finished my research project?'

Signor Minetti pressed my hand.

'You stay as long as you like, Claire. I'm sure that is what Paolo would want me to say. He was like a son to me, and you see, my dear, I know that he loved you.'

Toiling back through the slippery streets, in which bespattered citizens, in one gigantic display of solidarity, were engaged in moving muck from doorsteps, hallways and the gaping holes that a couple of days ago had been shops, I felt relieved that my whole being was not suffused with mourning. Paolo is no more, I told myself, now that the young Claire had withdrawn from the battlefield. And, of course, Paolo's sudden death now explained why my letters had come back, unopened, twenty years ago. An actor in the strangest of two-act plays, he had bowed out. So had the young Claire. And here I was, a survivor of a brief celebration of the senses, a Claire freed of those lecherous little devils that had burrowed themselves, tick-like, under my skin. And perhaps as a token of the catharsis that had taken place, I saw before me a glorious rainbow arching over the sky of my inner landscape, just as it stood in biblical times – as it was written – over the re-emerging land, as a witness to the Lord's Covenant.

12

Army and navy units were rolling in with water tanks and soup kitchens, just as my own supplies were running out. Soon I joined men and women plodding with buckets and containers through the jungle of sludge and debris, and through the smell of filth and naphtha.

Mechanical diggers, trucks, pumps, cranes and bulldozers arrived and they were greeted by the plagued locals like victorious forces. Losing no time, they shifted tree trunks, wrecked cars and piled-up trash; they scooped muck off the streets by the ton and drained flooded basements. The fire brigade distributed bread, Red Cross stations opened for First Aid and anti-typhoid injections. Deliveries of blankets, clothing and milk-powder allayed suffering.

Long, lonely, laboursome days, in which all that was good and strong and unselfish in me came to the fore, and which made my own dilemma, measured against the city's plight, appear trifling.

I now slept in the single bed in the spare room, seeing my move as much a symbolic act as an assurance that Paolo's nocturnal ghost would not claim his side of the mattress. Sometimes the emptiness of the flat, seen in things as little as the absence of Paolo's wet footmarks on the bathroom floor, or some carelessly discarded items of clothing, created a palpable vacuum. Besides, I had taken most of his personal effects to Signor Minetti, or stored them in the master bedroom, so that there now remained no more of Paolo in the kitchen and living-room than faint echoes of laughter and scraps of conversation and gestures. And if in languid moments memories of the intimate kind should flash through my mind, they found no lasting foothold.

Eleven days following the inundation of the city, the lights came back on, and water – though not fit for drinking – dripped from the taps. Florentines heaved sighs of relief, as daily life picked up by degrees – a life still dominated by *il fango maledetto,* and by the sticky, black oil which settled on the porous stone walls as indelible tidemarks, promising to remind people of The Flood for decades to come.

The river was still running high and evil-coloured between the Lungarni, when the first bold-letter notices appealing for volunteers were posted on the doors of churches, museums, libraries and archives. This was the signal I had been waiting for, and I acted upon it as I would have to any emergency.

Wearing Paolo's pullover, rubber boots, a green plastic apron, yellow washing-up gloves and my red-and-white dotted headscarf, I reported to the Biblioteka Nazionale, where I knew the sorry state of ancient books and manuscripts in the basement – among them a thousand volumes dating back to the sixteenth century – would bring tears to the eyes of historians, bibliographers and book buffs the world over. I also realised that a speedy salvage operation was imperative, if the mud-caked pages were to be saved from glueing inseparably together into a pulp.

For days I worked alongside soldiers, library personnel,

local students and men of letters in the damp and foul-smelling bowels of the Biblioteka, my feet stuck ankle-deep in sludge. I pulled books from the mud, or formed part of a human chain passing on each volume, to be loaded into army trucks and taken to one of the numerous places designated 'drying stations'. Like the rest of the salvage workers, I got splashed, freckled and daubed with mud. But I did not mind. I had found my role in a twentieth-century drama. I had also embarked on what I came increasingly to see as 'my long way home'.

Like a collector handling a rare book, I was scraping mud off a soiled tome one morning, when an English news team, backed up by a photographer, turned up in the Biblioteka. A camera, focused on the devastation, discovered me behind my defaced treasure.

'May I take a photograph of you, miss?'

'What, like this?' I cried, looking down on my mud-splattered boots, trousers and apron, and trying in vain to brush an encrusted strand of hair out of my face.

The camera clicked. The photographer's satisfied smile flashed at me.

'Great!' he roared. 'An English girl right in the muck of things. The editor will love it.'

Quietly, I carried on with my salvage work, but wondering what happens to a photograph taken in Florence at a time which had seen me in London, with Charles about to break my emotional deadlock.

Once the bulk of the damaged books had been shifted to 'laundering' and restoration sites, I went to work at the railway heating plant, one of the 'hospitals' for book casualties. Here we were presently joined by students of all nationalities – long-haired, bearded beatniks, clean-shaven sporting types and pale, bespectacled youths. A wild collection of volunteers we were, but we all had one thing in common: a love of books and respect for the legacy of learning – passions espoused to a strong sense of horror at the defilement under our hands, sentiments with which my own identified.

Undaunted by the sheer magnitude of books to be restored, we set to work, cleaning, sawdusting, washing the pages of each book, before hanging it over a line for drying. Sweat-shop fatigue. Multi-lingual invectives, sing-song, and jokes cracked light-heartedly over some despairing sight. Young people attempting to communicate with each other in their own vernacular or in English. Like other students involved in the city's gargantuan clean-up operation we were soon labelled 'Angels of the Mud', and I was proud to be one of them. It was, however, their fellowship – to which they admitted my pretty, trouser-clad self – which eased my sense of isolation, bolstered up my morale and restored a vanishing point to my perspective.

'What does the city look like these days?' I asked Margo, an English-and-History student from London, and she lost no time, launching into a portrayal of a capital in which Rudolf Nureyev was captivating ballet audiences, international ice-skaters were pirouetting at Olympia, and mini-skirted Twiggies parading their legs at the side of psychedelic-looking men in the King's Road.

'And just before I left London,' she said, 'the city and the south-east were hit by a hell of a gale.'

How far London was for me in terms of time, and how distant, like an astral body, Britain's capital in the sixties.

With some difficulty I tore myself away from my information-gathering and parallel musings, and invited Margo back to the flat for canneloni and a glass of wine. Over coffee that night I listened to my guest's tales of undergraduate life, one of wild parties and daredevil pranks, the kind which is often acknowledged to be part of a university education, but not necessarily confined – I remember all too well – to arts students.

Margo was easy to listen to. But it was the Chaplinesque manner in which she delivered her narrative which soon had me in stitches. For when it came to recounting a particularly off-beat or risqué episode, she emerged as a born comedienne and, at the end of our unassuming meal, as a fluffy dessert topped with cream.

'You're just what the doctor ordered,' I cried, between laughing spasms, just as not long ago Paul, doing a parody of a golfing duel with his father, had had a side-splitting effect on Charles and myself. It suddenly seemed a long time since I had appeared on Paolo's doorstep, confused, excited, key in hand; a long time since the sounds of levity had echoed through the flat, in which – thanks to Signor Minetti's generosity – I was living rent-free. Yet every day, in unguarded moments, my consciousness was still jumping eagerly and light-footed across the fence of Time. Thus it was that Margo caught me unawares.

'Here, have a fag,' she said, offering me an Embassy.

'No, thank you. I gave up twenty years ago,' I replied.

Margo looked dumbfounded.

'What do you mean? Did you start smoking in the cradle?'

I could not have felt worse than if I had been found guilty of an outright lie. Trying to make light of my blunder, I said:

'What I meant was that it feels positively ages since I gave it up.' But oh, how I itched to tell her that I had done so when I got married, and that over the last twenty years medical evidence had firmly established a connection between smoking and lung cancer.

My reply appeared to satisfy Margo, for she lit her cigarette with the dying flame of her match and embarked upon a subject matching her youth and quicksilver personality. However, when a few minutes later, I inadvertently made an all-too-knowing observation on London life in the eighties, and Margo's eyes jerked up in the face of the obviously preposterous, I took the plunge.

'What would you say, Margo, if I told you that I really belong to the Eighties? That I am a forty-four-year-old wife and mother, the victim of a metaphysical phenomenon, and that through a feat of my imagination I had landed myself back in the time of the flood?'

I was taking a gamble, but then I had really nothing to lose, apart from casting doubts on the soundness of my mind.

This time Margo's eyes held an element of fear, which she tried to mask with jocularity.

'What, a time traveller? Well, my dear, I'd say you'd read *The Time Machine* once too often, you were sloshed, or positively bonkers.' And rising hastily, 'It's getting late. I must be off. Thanks for the grub, it was great. See you tomorrow in the sweatshop.'

When she had gone, I suddenly felt acutely alone.

The Piazza Santa Maria Novella had been cleared of flood-smashed vehicles, tree trunks and the rubbish tips formed by the grimy litter of shop contents. The time had come, I reckoned, to investigate the state of Ucello's 'Deluge', and thus the chances of negotiating my passage back to my own time.

I slipped unobserved through the iron gate and down the steps to the cloister, prepared for, but not immune to, the sight that greeted me. Soldiers armed with shovels and scrapers were still slogging away at clearing yellowish mud from the inner courtyard and colonnades. The four cypresses cornering the quadrangle stood rigid, pyramidal, their lower halves tainted, as if dipped into molasses. Along the walls, a black tidemark reached a ten-foot level. Rhythmically, a pump coughed up sludge water into the Piazza through a hose, spades pitched mud into wheelbarrows, boots laboured through the mire. With my senses sharpened to the chill and dampness of the place, my legs proceeded, peacock-fashion, to the fresco. And there it was: The masterpiece, my hopeful catalyst. Or better, what little there was visible of it under its oil-stained muck.

The implications made me feel faint, and I leaned for support against a filthy column, my mind reeling: Was I to remain a captive of Time, with what I felt sure was my only escape route blocked? What would I do for money, now that my last lire were running out and the young Claire's sterling cheques were no longer coming in? And how could I explain yet another extension of my stay in Florence and in Paolo's flat to a generous Signor Minetti?

A curatorial voice momentarily repaired my composure. 'Signorina, the cloister is closed!'

The young, broad-skulled attendant, dressed in overalls and Wellingtons, stalked towards me with the officious mien of a major-domo.

'Oh, it's you, lady?' he cried, his face broadening, his carious incisors flashing recognition at me. 'Are you feeling better? I thought you looked like a ghost the last time you were here . . . behaved rather oddly, I might say. I was quite worried.'

'A virus infection,' I lied. 'It made me feel dizzy, and I thought I'd pass out. The antibiotic . . . '

'Ah, *i antibiotici!* An aunt of mine . . . '

'The fresco,' I interjected, pointing to Ucello's lunette, and with mourning in my voice, 'My God, what a mess!'

'*Si, si, terribile.*'

'It's a sacrilege . . . a desecration.'

The young Mussolini's head bobbed up and down in agreement.

'It will be restored,' I said, 'but it will take a long time.' My voice was close to a whine.

'*Si, si.*'

A little prompting revealed that experts, who were waiting for special salt solvents to arrive, would shortly attempt the removal of mud and oil stains, detach the fresco and take it to the refectory for restoration.

'It won't be back for months,' I stated flatly.

'I'm afraid not. It'll take months, perhaps years . . . '

'And the cloister?'

'It won't be open to the public for some time, not until we've cleared the place up.'

I looked suitably down-hearted.

'And I thought I could come in here now and again, once the worst of the muck had been chucked out . . . just to stroll around for a few minutes. The stillness in here, you see . . . '

The attendant's face registered the regret of a cinema commissionaire refusing a juvenile entry to an adult movie.

'If I let you in, signorina, I could get into trouble. We have our directives . . . Anyway, it wouldn't be much fun for you. The smell, for one, won't go quickly, and it'll take weeks to wash the oil off the masonry.'

'What's your name?' I asked.

'Luigi.'

I played my one and only trump card.

'Well, Luigi,' I began, and with all modesty explained that I was one of the 'Angels of the Mud', working on the salvage and restoration of books and manuscripts at the nearby railway heating plant.

'The heat and humidity there easily sap one's energy,' I said. 'I had hoped to escape to the cloister, whenever I feel like a dose of tranquillity and a refuelling of energy – that is, once the colonnade is passable again and the noisy machinery has gone.'

My disclosure had the effect of a generous tip.

'*Un angelo di fango!*' Luigi exclaimed, as if I had revealed that I was blood-related to the British royal family, or was going steady with Paul McCartney. 'Well, in that case I'll be happy to let you in when I'm on duty. After all, we owe a great debt to you foreign students. Even the papers say you people are a hell of lot better than your reputation. It just shows you, one should never judge students by the way they dress or by the length of their hair.'

I agreed, and to ingratiate myself further, commented on the hard toil the mud-clearing involved. Then I bade the guardian of the cloister a most genial 'ciao' and ploughed through a channel of nauseous-looking water back to the exit. I knew I would need a lot of patience, until the cloister could become a place of pilgrimage for me again. But how would I deal with the terrifying, mocking bareness of the fresco wall?

On my way back to the heating plant I wondered whether it was worth mending the elbows of Charles' green cardigan, which were rather threadbare, or whether I should make him part with it, by buying a new one, perhaps for Christmas. I thought about my washing-machine, which was making strange noises on its 'Delicates' programme, and that I had better let someone have a look at it. That is, once I got home. Oh, God, if ever . . . !

13

A stiff December wind was sweeping across the roofs of the city. Many museums reopened, shop windows displayed goods from Christmas tinsel to Limoges china and Milan fashions, and shopping for groceries no longer conjured up images of war-time shortages. Drinking water came back and in some quarters gas. The first staggering tallies of art treasures lost or spoiled emerged, as did figures of people drowned or missing in the flood. Although pumps were still in evidence in the worst-affected areas of the city, it was now a pleasure to be able to walk through the streets without soiling one's shoes.

The day the telephone started working again, Signor Minetti called to say that his wife's condition had improved and he was taking her to their villa in Fiesole for a prolonged rest and a change of scene. I was not to worry about the flat, just to look after it as a good friend would do. He added instructions as to what to do with the key of the apartment if and when I was ready to leave the city. And, of course, I would be welcome at the villa any time.

But I knew I would not want to pay another visit to the lovely hillside villa, where Paolo had been born and memories of him would be enshrined. I knew I would not want to walk in a garden again, which in spring had been drenched with scents, in summer been riotous with colour, and which now, in the darkest month of the year, would be sombre with evergreens. No laughter would echo from the moss-infested stone walls, no lovers' whispers rise out of its secluded spots. The breath of dead chrysanthemums, damp soil and decay in urns and terracotta pots would prevail, an odour which always reminded me of late-November cemeteries and mortality. And I could just see the two cypresses standing on either side of the gate, darkly, like undertakers offering a welcome to a hall of mourning . . .

The functioning telephone before me, I was unable to resist the temptation to dial London again. Would I get through? Would the voice at the other end be that of the sixties or, weirdest notion of all, of the eighties? I immediately rejected the latter as something that might strain even a Wellesian imagination and lifted the receiver.

But once again my effort to establish a link with the world as I knew it failed – a world which, aged by twenty years, had seen the death of dictators, earthquakes, civil wars, the invasion of Czechoslovakia, the exchange of eastern and western spies, British decimal coinage and the enthronement of Margaret Thatcher as prime minister, to name but a few incidents of world-shaking or national importance, if not such locally monumental events as Switzerland giving its women the vote.

Once again, too, it was hammered home to me that I was being detained at King Time's pleasure. I felt incarcerated in a dimension of time in which I did not belong, and in which even the voice of what poets and minstrels once called 'my own true love' was beyond my reach.

It was twelve days before Christmas.

* * *

I was now working at the Uffici as part of an art-student team, imbued with a singleness of purpose that affected anyone handling paintings ravished by mud and oil-stained water.

Brushing a damaged frame, cleaning a soiled masterpiece or sieving muck for the hopeful presence of ancient flakes of paint, I felt strangely distanced from the spiritual and material manifestations of the season. By the time I got back to the flat, I was usually too tired to go out and socialise, and as my money was running out fast, I could not afford to eat out.

Yet my solitude after dark did not disturb me, not while Vivaldi's 'Four Seasons' or a Mozart concerto formed the euphonious background to Dante's *Vita Nova*, Petrarca's lyricism or an escapist novel. Perhaps the thought that I was serving out a kind of sentence helped me to devise a modus vivendi and cope with the shadows beyond the beam of my lamp.

Sometimes, seeing my face in the bathroom mirror, I would pray that the glass would suddenly mist over and, wiped clear, reveal more familiar features, lines and all. That it would reflect the greenish, marble-patterned tiles of my London bathroom, the matching shower curtains, and on the door my white bathrobe, on which the hanger was coming loose. But fixedly and prolonged as I might stare at my younger image, hard as my breath plastered hazy film over the glass, it would not change.

Sometimes I shuddered at the knowledge that was mine only, and that I could never communicate to the hopeful explorers of Time and Dimensions; the knowledge which in the absence of data to back it up, would not only generate scepticism but blatant displeasure at what scientists might see as an attempt to waste their precious time, and the tabloids would wish to exploit like the sighting of a spaceship – that is, if I ever got back.

There were times when I found myself engaged in morbid monologues, or when I came close to outbursts of frustration. There were nights when sleep played truant. Or when, as soon as I had put out the light, or some unfamiliar noise woke me in the fragile hours, my thoughts would journey home.

One such night, mounting crystal-clear images, and luring me even olfactorily, my mind played back the familiar pre-Christmas scene: the cosiness of the living-room, now graced by a blazing Ponsietta and a thick-bellied vase sprouting twigs of pine-coned fir and mistletoe. The smell of butter and cinnamon cookies, wafting from the kitchen. Charles calling from his armchair retreat, 'What about a glass of hot punch, darling?' And there is my own contented self, buying Christmas presents at Harrods and Marks & Spencer, stocking up the larder and lining up, on the mock Adam mantelpiece, Christmas cards and invitations for festive drinks. In the corner by the window a Christmas tree completes the nostalgic picture: a spiky Norwegian spruce, decorated so as not to obscure the sated green of its robe, nor choke its pine scent . . .

On waking next morning I felt my morale cracking, and I had to summon up my innermost strength, not to fall apart.

It was the day I decided to pay another visit to the Green Cloister.

As had lately been my custom, I sat down on the low parapet opposite the stone wall, from which Ucello's fresco had been detached. The light around me was poor, the air damp and chilly, compounded with an odour which did not invite one to linger. There was no one about, and Luigi, the attendant, was keeping to his cubicle by the gate, close to an electric fire.

My eyes fastened on the emptiness before me, as they would on the Holy Shroud in Turin, had the world's most sophisticated tests confirmed as genuine the piece of linen, in which the body of Christ was believed to have been wrapped.

Bare, greyish-brown stone stared back at me, stone mesmerizing with its nakedness, and as vacuous as my mind, now that the hushed calm of the cloister had filtered out the cacophony of the streets. Stone as potent in its effect on my inner receptiveness as a florid high altar to a worshipper . . .

I am growing oblivious to my surroundings, except for the cooing of a pigeon on the roof above me. As I sit, spinning a drugged haze around me, the wall is suddenly taking on a life of its own. Slowly, its pores open wide, exuding beads of moisture. Air bubbles form, billow, burst, before miniature jets of steam spew forth, geyser-like. Stone quivers, as it broils under its nudity and relieves itself of built-up pressure. And now, in a striking change of the stone's behaviour, the spouting ceases, moisture evaporates, and out of the wall's epidermal craters colours rise to the surface – a mélange of bluish-grey, yellow, orange, shades of greens and browns, colours as anaemic in tone as the artist might have intended them or as the centuries left them. Colours running, oozing, foaming, bubbling; colours wriggling to freedom like maggots or bleeding into mural tissue as petechiae. And they all fight for spatial dominance. Here, rivulets of orange join brown drifts, to form an ark-coloured hue, there yellow streaks soak up grey tints or liaise with blue ones, before claiming their place. While, amid the great struggle and relocationing, blobs of green divide, cell-like, into serene units.

Gradually, colours are fashioning objects and defining

contours. The last globules attach themselves to their own kind. Stone sighs, cools off, closes its pores.

Since my eyes are glued to the lower part of the lunette which is beginning to manifest itself, my eyes are spared the flood scene so disturbingly evoked in the upper part of the fresco. And that is why I now witness the bearded patriarch, Noah, stretching his hand out towards the dove as it returns, a leafy twig in its bill. All around, the waters have receded, and the ark is lying serenely aground. Trees take on shape, so does the hump of a hill, a vine-clad trellis. Figures, spectral in their washed-out paint, crowd the foreground. And now, God, the Father, materialises in the sky. Leaning out of the clouds as from a window, haloed by a giant rainbow arching over the landscape, He is speaking to Noah and his sons of His Covenant with men, and of the rainbow being His token of such Covenant. And so powerful is the happening before me, so poignant the message it imparts, that the redressed stone seems to breathe the Almighty's very words at me, the onlooker:

'And it shall come to pass, when I bring a cloud over the earth, that a bow shall be seen in the cloud . . . '

14

'Signora!'

The voice reached me as from across biblical times.

'*Stiamo chiudendo*. We're closing, lady! The cloister will open again in the afternoon.' The voice was firm and husky. It was solicitous. 'Signora, are you feeling all right?'

I stared at Persil-white dentures, and at a squarish bald pate, which, once again, conjured up an instant image of the famous Mussolini skull. Towering over me was the stocky, uniformed figure of the attendant, whose girth bespoke of a fondness for pasta and long siestas. And now my heart jumped as my eyes fell on my tailored suit, my low-heeled leather shoes and modish handbag – the apparel that went with the Claire I knew best, and who had been sent to Florence to do a job. I touched my hair, which was short and stylishly cut. I looked at my left hand as if it were a mirror. Here, at last was the final proof: a wedding ring sitting next to a humble-sized diamond.

My smile was one of mad rejoicing. I felt like putting my arms around 'Mussolini', like waltzing along the Colonnade, like shouting 'Hurrah!'.

'*Sta bene?*' The attendant repeated, rattling a bunch of keys.

'*Si, si,*' I cried. 'Yes, thank you, I'm all right. I think my mind strayed a bit. Somehow, I was far away. The fresco . . . '

'Ah, not a rare thing in here,' revealed my man. 'Visitors often find this particular one playing tricks with their imaginaton. Some of them come back year after year. They say no other fresco or painting haunts them so much, or contains such a strong . . . eh, emotion. Of course, there's not much detail left . . . '

'How long have you been the custode?

'Well over twenty years. I first came when . . . '

' . . . and your name is Luigi?'

'Si. But how come you know my name?'

'I don't,' I lied. 'It just seems to fit you.'

I got up, pressed a few lire notes into the warden's hand and made rapidly for the exit. A last glance back at the fresco, a nod to the faint tidemark running alongside the colonnade walls, and at the metal plaque, high up, which marked the flood level in sixty-six. I thought the grass looked thirsty, and that the cypresses, their lower trunks no longer tainted the colour of treacle, peaked happily into the soft luminosity of the midday sky.

'*Gracie*, signora,' called a voice after me. 'I suppose I shall see you again.'

'You won't,' I cried, glancing back. 'Not for a long while.'

His puzzled stare followed me out of the cloister.

I saw her the moment I stepped into the Piazza. Surrounded by an ever-greedy flock of pigeons, her head and shoulders arched forward, her lips forming cooing sounds, the Lady in Grey threw a last morsel of breakfast roll to the birds, straightened up and neatly folded her paper bag away. I experienced a feeling akin to affection for her, an urge to run towards this heartening symbol of the eighties. In a style befitting my age, I was about to cross over to her, introduce myself as her fellow coach passenger and offer a few pleasantries, when a platoon of Japanese, impatiently welcoming some stragglers leaving the church, positioned itself in my field of vision, thus obliterating the Grey Lady from my sight. By the time I had bypassed the tourists she was walking away, looking neither right nor left, her head held up high. And there was no frailty in her gait, no arthritic economy of movement, other than a suggestion that she had achieved her objective.

My mouth was dry and thirsting for a coffee. But I felt too impatient, too reluctant to waste time over a creature comfort, when I could further establish my identity at the hotel. I studied my image in a shop window. That's better, I thought, contours with which I am familiar. Nothing can go wrong now. And I don't need a newspaper to ascertain the year. Yet, if I am honest, and who could blame me under the circumstances, there remained an iota of uncertainty in my mind. Was I perhaps up against another trick of Time?

The hotel's modern interior instantly put my mind at rest. So did the middle-aged, raven-haired receptionist who greeted my hurried entrance with the raised eyebrows of proprietorial concern.

'Back so soon, signora? *Tutt' é bene?*'

'Yes, yes,' I cried, 'everything is all right. I forgot something.' In the champagne mood in which I found myself I spoke of the chances of leaving my head behind one day, which elicited a sisterly smile and made the lady reach for my room key. And I could not help grinning at the gilt-framed Venetian mirror, which, in response, seemed to wink at me, or being fascinated, most ungraciously, by the ultimate proof of my return to the eighties: the woman's mole, which had grown with its host, and which sprouted two long dark hairs that twitched with every movement of her lips.

Back in my room, the mirror beckoned. Breathless, self-critical, yet with the affection one accords to one's outer shell, no matter what shape or age, I took stock of my figure. I surveyed my broadened hips, the crow-feet of easy smiles, the gentle furrows of hard thinking, animated speech and commitment, the facial witnesses also to the peaks and abysses in my life. Hello! I said to my visual chronicler. Glad you're back.

And now that I felt firmly restored to my own time, I grew soft inside like mushy fruit. Something behind my sternum swelled and strained and ached, wanting out, until I could bear it no longer. I sat down by the telephone and dialled.

'Hello, Charles,' I said, the receiver trembling in my hand. Not so much that I was overcome by the final proof of there existing, beyond the city's boundaries, a private world that was my own, but because there was nothing I wanted more at that very moment than to hear the voice which not long ago – according to my manipulated inner calendar – had been light years away from me.

'Claire, is that you, darling?'

The voice. Soft, affectionate, solicitous. The voice that had never played a Trumpet Voluntary, but chamber music, and in our most intimate communications, a violin solo. Suddenly I was a teenager again, ringing a hopeful date, or the young Claire calling Charles the day after I had finally realised that I had fallen in love again.

'Yes, Charles, it's me.' The precursors of tears throttled my gullet.

'This is a surprise. Had a good flight?'

'Yes, thank you.'

'Hotel all right?'

'Yes, fine.'

A long pause.

'Claire, are you still there?'

I breathed a 'yes' into the mouthpiece.

'Darling, is something wrong?'

'No.' I was choking. The seconds were ticking away. Charles, however, remained silent, giving me time. How it humiliated me, how it caressed me across the miles . . .

'Charles,' I began.

'Yes, darling.'

'I love you.'

'I'm sorry, I can't hear you, the line is bad.'

'I said *I love you*,' I shouted into the instrument, tears streaming down my face. I was conscious of my declaration of love taking Charles aback, of making him stare at the receiver in his hand, as if lines were crossed. Of emotions unfolding in him and struggling out of their reserve, feelings never aired in the middle of the day or over the telephone, and certainly not when he was sitting at his departmental desk, perhaps a cup of cold coffee beside him or such mundane objects as students' essays, a draft for a public lecture or a memo from the University Senate.

Silence floated between us, winged, a telecommunication of the spirit.

'Claire, are you still there?'

'Yes, Charles.'

'I love you, too, darling. Hurry back home. I miss you.'

I swallowed hard, being suffused with a sense of longing and belonging, with the warmth of mulled wine drunk on a wintry night in front of an open fire.

Charles must have understood, for he did not query my renewed silence.

'I'm afraid I must go,' he continued. 'Students are knocking on my door. I've got a tutorial. Voltaire. We'll be examining Candide's cynical indifference to his misfortunes.'

I smiled under my tears.

'That should make for an interesting session,' I said. 'Goodbye, then.'

'G'bye for now. Take care, darling. See you soon.'

I slowly replaced the receiver.

Everything was back in focus.

And more.

15

As I walked out into the late-autumn sunshine – for the second time that day, so my inner clock told me – my sortie to the sixties struck me increasingly as no more than a figment of the imagination. But whether fantasy or not, my hyped-up desire to track Paolo down or, at best, soil my mental picture of him, had suddenly punctured like a balloon. At the same time I knew that I would not have to inspect the city's record for the names of persons killed during the flood, or missing, presumed drowned. And weirdest of all, that my intimate knowledge of the disaster and its aftermath could only have been that of a witness.

For once reason stamped its foot like an *enfant terrible*. It said: No post mortem, no feasibility study, if you please. All that matters now is that you have laid the young Paolo to rest, and that the Florence of the Eighties, complete with its commemorative sideshows, is yours to explore.

And so I worked my way through the city traffic which, in the main thoroughfares pounded as relentlessly as in rush-hour London, Paris or Rome. Neither did the alleys provide relief in muted sound. Walking along a strip of pavement not wide enough to let oncoming pedestrians pass, I was startled out of my wits every time a moped or scooter darted out from behind or accelerated into a vacant space ahead. Exhaust fumes poisoned the air, trapped it in the chasms of the streets. In the absence of a fanning breeze, it hung like a poisonous cloud over the Piazza del Duomo, where packaged tourists, touts, begging gypsies, and youths ear-plugged to transistor radios, swarmed about like ants or moved in viscous counter-currents, surrounded by the roaring tide of traffic, and overlooked – with the forbearance and impotence of wise old men – by Brunelleschi's majestic cathedral and Giotto's Campanile.

Shoppers and cruising tourists thronged the main streets, high-decibel multi-lingual confabulation strained against the din of the traffic, while culturally keen crowds filed patiently into the bowels of museums or stepped into the hushed semi-darkness of churches, reverently, airily or as if mentally ticking off another guidebook recommendation.

Comparisons presented themselves, graphic memories which so far were withholding verification: the sound of a swirling, snarling current of filthy water, the awesome stillness of streets and public squares flooded or clogged with mud; the sight of gutted shops, the defilement of façades, ancient paint, fabric, books and documents. And as if sculptured in my mental hall of recall, the grim faces of mud-spattered Florentines, salvaging, cleaning up and restoring their lives to normality by degrees. Pictures so lucid, sounds so distinctive, impressions so incompatible with mere fantasy.

The day's itinerary urged me on.

In the Piazza della Signoria a Combined Forces exhibition commemorated the twentieth anniversary of the flood. The famous square, in which Savonarola, the eloquent fifteenth-century preacher and revolutionary, was burnt at the stake for heresy, and which during most of the day and throughout the best part of the year groaned under the hordes of foreign sightseers, now held amphibian vehicles, heavy pumping and salvaging equipment, a motorized soup kitchen, a Red Cross station, a helicopter, a fire-brigade rescue vehicle and a drinking water tank on wheels – units deployed during the flood and in its muddy wake. On billboards, photographs, newspaper cuttings, and blown-up aerial maps marking the extent of the flood, invited closer inspection. All the while, members of the Combined Services stood waiting, to impart information to younger citizens and visitors on the role the various teams had played in those days.

It was all there: copious copy-writing material, a strong background invocation of the flood. But no questions came to my lips. According to my inner eye I had seen it all before. Whether pumps, diggers or soup kitchens, I had watched them all in operation. Had I not?

New doubts sprouted their importune heads. Incredulity and rational thinking repudiated the possibility of a *déjavu*, of having been the victim of a jest of Time. And yet, how could I disprove experiences ingrained in my memory, and as projectable as my graduation or my wedding-day, or as that terrible morning when Paul, following an operation for a burst appendix and symptoms of peritonitis, was fighting for his life. When in a moment of privacy I had knelt before my God, imploring Him to save my son's life?

Once again I resolved to let matters rest until I had put the Channel between Florence and myself. In a landscape of things comprehensible and verifiable, theories about things incomprehensible and unverifiable surely shape up more easily.

In front of the Palazzio Vecchio, the giant copy of Michelangelo's 'David' spurned the eyes of tourist voyeurs. I thought his face reflected a shade of disgust, not so much because his magnificent nakedness was on show like a crucified body, or his genitalia proved to be one of the main attractions for salacious-minded visitors. Not so much because a mixture of polluted air and rain had streaked his face and the inside of one thigh a nauseous brownish black, but because some disrespecting lager or chianti lout had varnished his toenails crimson. But there was no time to muse about the whims of night-revellers and man's environmental contempt. I fortified myself with a coffee and a brioche, and set off on a round of churches, chapels and museums, a trek commensurate with a pilgrimage.

In the Santa Croce Museum I stood before Cimabue's partly restored, partly permanently damaged Cross – as before a shrine. And I liked to think that it was no coincidence, when at that very moment a ray of sunshine fell through a nearside window and on to the Cross, and I was alone in the big hall with the poignancy of the sunlit crucified figure of Christ. In the adjacent chapel and church I marvelled that none but the ubiquitous, if faint, tidemarks on walls and tombs and stone columns were left to remind the sharp-eyed visitor of the one-time agony of the sacred.

Several taxi rides later, I had seen many of the paintings, statues and altar-pieces which had been severely damaged in the flood. I had spoken to custodians, curators, restorers and librarians; I had interviewed the editor of *La Nazionale*, who insisted that I watch a short cine-film of *L'Alluvione* in the newspaper's auditorium. The film effectively evoked the dramatic events for viewers ignorant of the extent of the disaster, and – judging by the excited chatter of elderly Italians in the audience – it stirred up uneasy memories for some. Bombarding my own mind with pictures reeling back from the past, it strongly supported my theory of a previous experience.

I tracked down two antiquarians who looked as if they

had been in business twenty years ago. Asked if they remembered an English girl warning them of a devastating flood to come, they both professed a lapse in memory. Perhaps they had been in the stockroom at the time, or taking care of other business, they suggested. Had they conveniently forgotten the incident, I wondered, or were they loth to admit that a *straniera* had pleaded with them to take precautionary measures?

But the official part of my day was not over yet. Suffice to say that I managed to speak to a group of students who deplored the absence of a spirit of solidarity in the society of the eighties, the kind of unity and team spirit, they said, which their parents and grandparents had experienced at the time of the flood; I interviewed older citizens in shops, doorways and bus queues, who cursed the memory of *il fango mostro* and praised the same *spirito del solidarita* which had briefly united Florentines in a classless muck-fighting society. And none forgot to mention the unselfish efforts of the Angels of the Mud, which against my better judgement made me feel as if my back was being patted.

My notebook was full. My legs felt like lead, my head inflated with information, visual confrontation, street noise and fumes. As Paul would have put it, I was whacked. I longed for a bath, a change of clothes and a large gin and tonic. But then the sunset promised to be a nostalgic one. Already the light was tinting pink, and a bluish mist veiled the distant hills. Time for a quick visit to the Ponte Vecchio.

The goldsmiths' and jewellers' shops were still open. Although some of them had acquired a different, often less sophisticated look, and a few shops now qualified as souvenir boutiques geared towards the less discerning tourist, I found the familiar entrance and shop surround to be still of polished, brass-mounted wood and the window still elegantly dressed.

A young assistant greeted me with a smile which dropped, shutter-like, when I turned out to have no customer potential.

'Of course, I was not here at the time,' he said, a trifle tartly, as if I suspected him of being an old man in his forties. 'Perhaps the present owner will be able to help you.

He went into the back room and fetched an elderly gentleman whom my enquiries took readily back to the sixties.

'Ah, Signor Minetti . . . Of course I remember him. I bought his business in the seventies. He died a few years later. His wife, I believe passed away in the late sixties.'

'And their grandson, Paolo? He used to work here.' The question glided smoothly over my lips.

'A fine young man. Very good looking and quite a wizard with his hands he was. Oh yes, I remember him well. *Que peccato!* What a pity . . . '

'Why, what happened to him?'

'Poor chap was washed out of the shop at the height of the flood in sixty-six, they say. He was never found. *Una tragedia . . . '*

Just then a customer entered and looked around to be served. Taking my cue, I thanked the signor and left.

Why, I asked myself, did I require confirmation of Paolo's death? Does one have to see a grave, in order to be convinced of a person's demise?

Flowing sluggishly, its muddy colour injected with faint rose tints, and with a shaft of reddish gold in mid-channel, the Arno's untroubled mood belied that its waters could ever swell into a fierce current, breaking embankments and deluging a city. That it could ever be driven as if cursed by an angry god, to damage, destroy and claim human sacrifices.

As I stood under the *belle-vue* arch of the bridge, my face turned up-river towards the misted-over fireball, I half expected a voice to spring up behind me: 'A beautiful sunset, signorina, isn't it?' But the sound of constant stop-go traffic on the Lungarno, carried across the water by a stiff November breeze, the appreciative comments of tourists, cameras clicking away at my elbows and a group of loud-mouthed punkish types professing, through loutish behaviour, contempt for the edifying aspect before them, cut short any further recall and thwarted what I had intended as a silent soliloquy which would stand as an epitaph over Paolo's watery grave.

I hastened off the bridge as if vandals were at work in a cemetery.

I slept soundly that night, exhausted from the day's investigative marathon, my soul restored with a robust meal in my 'chummy' restaurant, and my thirst for a verification of the past quenched by more wine than was good for me.

When I woke next morning, gusts of wind were rattling the shutters and the dull light filtering through suggested overcast skies, all of which tempted me to turn over. But no such indulgences were mine that morning which beckoned with a programme devoted entirely to my aesthetic pleasures, while the afternoon prescribed one last chore as the final coffin nail to my private assignment.

After breakfast I turned art-hungry tourist. I revisited Michelangelo's 'Piétà', Cellini's 'Perseus' and Taddeo Gaddi's 'Last Supper'; I rubbed elbows with wide-eyed admirers of Botticelli's 'Primavera', soaked up the golden colours in Titian's 'Flora' and spent devotional moments at the altar of other favourite canvases, sculptures and triptychs – moments which, familiar to many art lovers – breed thoughts akin to prayer.

Following an early snack lunch which, for convenience, I took at one of the new self-serve restaurants geared to tourists and a quick turnover, rather than to a gourmet's palate, I armed myself with a raincoat and umbrella and bought a rail ticket to Viareggio. Time, I thought, for a final confrontation with the past, time to prove that I would not succumb to nostalgia, but demonstrate to myself, that like the Thyrrenean sea resort, I had moved on to another season.

16

Conditions at Viareggio were ideal for another cold douche of realism, which confirmed my view that any stark visual or atmospheric change of place that has once touched one's sensibilities so deeply as to claim a part of oneself, has an anaemic, if not lethal, effect on images cherished over the years.

In the sapping of my own quality of recall that afternoon, the weather certainly did its damnedest to play along. Having matured to gale force, the westerly wind was whipping up the sea which, a far cry from its picture-postcard image, had turned the colour of steel, its unruly waves, here and there, being toned up by whitish spume. Even the temperature had dropped a few degrees.

The small town, which I remembered as a sleepy summer retreat, had spread vigorously along its coastal stretches and into its hinterland. New summer houses, hotels, shops and roads were in evidence, some window displays had acquired a stylish look – tour operators had brought big business to Viareggio. Now, even the skyline had been manipulated by high-rise blocks of flats jutting out of the harmonious coastal panorama like tooth stumps and, intrusively, into the metallic hues of the Carrera mountains – the range of hills famed for their marble, and for taking on bluish tints under bright skies.

A blanket of variegated greys hung over the streets, to which the number of hotels, shops and private residences shut for the winter, added their own note of cheerlessness. In tune with the town's somnolent mood, locals were emerging from their siesta hours as from a state of hibernation. A moped passed at low speed, a van moved along the main thoroughfare as if it were running on its last drop of petrol. No animated holiday voices or music spilled through the open doors of bars, no glasses chinked, no steam hissed from coffee machines.

Along the promenade, bathing huts, fast-food stalls, beach-chair huts and amusement arcades were locked up. So were the big seafront hotels which in their dormancy and in the bleak light looked much less grand and in need of an outer facelift. The resort had rid itself of holiday-makers and beachcombers, quick-lire operators, itinerant gelati vendors, weekend paparazzi and city louts. It had said arriverderci to foreign vowels, transistor blasts and traffic jams. And having holed itself up for the winter, its atmosphere intimated that neither the pounding of the sea, nor the screeching of hungry seagulls driven inland by the lack of beach scraps, would intrude upon its repose.

But another summer would come. Viareggio, like any other seaside town, would wake from its seasonal winks and once again prostitute itself to the seekers of sun, sand and sea, and to those requiring fun-fair entertainment, in order to dispel their ennui between roasting sessions. I had visions of hordes of semi-nude sunbathers packing the beach or strolling along the promenade under the unorchestrated blare of pop music. Of youths on mopeds treating the seafront road like La Monza racecourse, or tossing away cans and fast-food disposables with blatant unconcern. And I knew Viareggio would never be gracefully alive again, never again offer its beach to the sun-hungry as a privilege – as it had done in the days of my golden summer . . .

A few steps and I was on the beach, which was deserted but for a man walking his dog. I put up my coat collar, but withstood the temptation to tie my scarf over my head. For it was good to feel the squally wind tousling my hair aggressively and seemingly blowing right through my skull, bracing and purging. The thunder of the waves breaking ashore filled my ears with welcome sound. There was, after all, nothing like the passions of the elements to drive out the devil in one and leave an inner vista of calm and peace.

I walked gingerly through the sand which I had memorized as white and unspoiled, and which now had the colour of wet cement. And there was decidedly nothing pristine about the beach's lower stretches where the tide, before depositing frothy phlegm, was washing back or sucking away peach stones, orange peel, empty sun-oil bottles and other sad fragments of a tourist summer. Nor about its upper expanse which was littered with plastic petrol containers, broken glass, beer cans, lemonade bottles, condoms, grease-paper and wooden debris – eyesores which superimposed themselves facilely on my former images of the beach and on any remnant romantic associations, choking the breath out of them.

The smell of the sea was in my nostrils, a good, tonic smell which always made me think of billowing sails, equatorial skies and seafarers' tales, but also of forces primordial, unfettered and cruel, a salty smell which now slapped my olfactory nerves, preventing them from recalling the lush flowering scents that had once been drifting seawards on sultry summer nights.

I looked for the trattoria, for the pergola which used to provide shade in daytime, and under which – whenever moonlight dwelt on a glassy sea – lovers had spun their dreams to the sound of soft music or the sensuous strains of a mandolin.

I looked in vain.

In its place, close to umbrella pines, there now stood a seafood ristorante with a concrete terrace and the naked steel supports of an awning. Here I came across an impressionist still-life scene: a white plastic table left to winter in the open and rattling on its unstable legs each time a gust of wind tried to lift it as if it were a woman's skirt; a glass forced to the table's edge, empty but for the dregs of red wine and dead insects; an old newspaper stuck around one of its legs, flapping like a sail. Summer was over on Viareggio's beach, and only the staccato hammering of a roadside drill, and the monotonous booms of a pile-driver working away at a nearby building site, conjured up visions of next season's packed crowds.

Shivering by now, I hurried off the beach and looked for a place where I could warm up the inner woman. The medicine I had adminstered to myself had been a strong one, and I had swallowed it without creasing my nose, and in the knowledge that though unpalatable it was high in curative properties. Time then, I thought, for a hot coffee and a piece of Tuscan *torta*, time to sit and rest and filter the sounds of wind and sea out of my ears.

I found a table in a main-street *caffè-panettaria*, and for the next half hour allowed myself to sit back and let the sluggishness of town life rub off on me. I watched housewives chatting over their purchase of bread or cake as if they had all the time in the world; I gazed through the window at the odd vehicle passing in low gear, and at pedestrians who paced themselves as if they were killing time or subscribed to one of Anatole France's maxims, according to which:

'Time deals gently only with those who take it gently.'

And in the same spirit I lifted my cup and cake fork to my mouth.

Then I saw her.

Walking with her firm, purposeful steps, and easily identified by her horn-handle bag and the striking mousiness of her attire, she was approaching on the opposite side of the street, her eyes reaching through the café window, to rest on me. Or so it seemed. I brought my cup down hard and stared at the apparition. Questions zoomed through my head. Had my eyes been playing a trick on me? Had I been the victim of an optical delusion? Had I seen a phantom in broad daylight, one subconsciously launched by my mind which, buffeted by the wind and fronted by all-too-conspicuous seasonal contrasts and moribund images, had finally been lulled into a laudanum state?

But there, large as life, she was, on her face a Giaconda smile, inscrutable, yet suggesting that the recipient knew how to interpret it. And now, already beyond eye-contact, she squared her shoulders in that by now familiar mannerism and, looking straight ahead, continued on her way.

At last my so agreeably relaxed mood gave way to action. I jumped up, nearly upsetting my chair in the process, and attracting the startled look of shoppers. Out I rushed into the street. But I was too late. Hard as I looked, the Lady in Grey had disappeared.

Back at my table, I slowly drained my cup and forked up the last tasty morsels on my plate. And now it was I who smiled. For whether the lady had indeed been forsaking the delights of Florence for a wind-swept, yawning seaside resort, or whether her sudden appearance had been the product of my fertile imagination: I had understood.

I got back to Florence in time to shower, shampoo the salt out of my hair and rinse the sand from between my toes. Tired as I was I treated myself to a three-star restaurant dinner, washed down by a half bottle of Barolo and followed by *zabaglione*, the queen of Italian desserts. It had been a good day, I thought, strange but successful. Tomorrow I would have dinner at home, something out of the freezer and into the oven, or a quick English-style salad. Tomorrow I would sleep at Charles' side again, my inner clock reset, my blessings counted, and my expedition into the past, if rationally assessed, a mere phantasmagoria.

But there remained something else to be done, something that would bring my personal assignment to a poignant conclusion. And before I fell asleep that night I kept reminding myself: First thing tomorrow . . . as soon as the gate of the Ponte Vecchio opens . . .

17

A cold mist was shrouding the city when I awoke. I knew it would lift later in the morning, leaving the air clear and softening, before descending again in the afternoon, shot through with orange or rose tints, and nipping the air as a harbinger of winter. Tonight, back in London, Florence would be no more than a framed memory, just like its art treasures, the vernal delights of Fiesole and the sunset views from the Ponte Vecchio. Like the cypresses towering over the tranquillity of the Green Cloister's quadrangle, or the sight, blown up in my mind, of the dove returning from dry land in Ucello's fresco, a leafy symbolism of new life on earth in its beak. And, unframed, chaotic in its presentation, tangible only in heady moments, the memory of my own deluge.

I walked through the narrow, twisting lanes with a resolute gait, blind to the obscenity of graffiti and spray-painted slogans on walls, deaf to the explosive engine of a motorcycle and the clamouring bark of a dog, insensitive to the dank smell rising from mediaeval hallways and fissure-like apertures between buildings. A short cut led me past the dilapidated façades of flat-converted minor palazzi and Dickensian artisan shops, past wrought-iron gates opening up into courtyards, where a lime or chestnut tree might stretch its crown towards the light, and where terracotta urns were still awash with autumn's late bloom or summer-wilted tendrils.

At this early hour, the prestigious end of the Ponte was still free of guru-followers splashing their saffron presence about and drumming on tambourines; it was as yet blessedly unmolested by youths fashionably termed vandals or Visigoths by their elders, while the lower approach to the bridge, under Vasari's Corridor, was still waiting for painters to set up their easels.

In jewellers and goldsmiths' shops assistants were busy polishing windows or giving silver exhibits a morning shine. Nobody took notice of me and the red rose in my hand, and I said a silent prayer when I found the viewpoints under the central arches still devoid of crowds, the souvenir stall closed and no roving vendors plying an early trade.

I leaned over the parapet, looking downriver – a view not as much favoured by visitors to the city as its opposite, more photogenic aspect. This morning the Arno was flowing fast, and its yellow waters reflected the veiled light, while close to its northern piers it formed islands of sluggish, turbid currents. A river dressed to accept my last respects, a river ready to flush my floral tribute, down towards the sea like a wreath, as it would have swept Paolo to his grave twenty years ago.

As I threw my rose into an eddying drift, I was conscious of the gesture being the final act of a drama which had been interlaced with black comedy and elements of surrealism.

'Farewell, my love,' I whispered, then walked off the bridge, with my bearing reflecting the accomplishment of a vital goal.

And I rejoiced in the great calm settling over me.

18

The coach journey to Pisa lent itself to the overture of final stocktaking. In vain I had waited for the Lady in Grey to board, hoping that she might also be bound for home, and keeping for her the seat next to me. I felt disappointed, cheated out of the opportunity to rub elbows with her, engage her in conversation and thus expunge the mystique about her. But any regrets at being denied her very real proximity evaporated rapidly, and by the time I was airborne, and sipping a glass of complimentary Asti Spumante, she was no more than a spectral figure who had briefly crossed my path.

As always when flying, the altitude generated in me a feeling of clear-headed detachment. And this now suggested the drawing-up of a balance-sheet. I knew that Paolo's spirit would no longer haunt me, nor his image torture me in a foreplay to lovemaking. In this I had achieved my goal. More significantly, something orgiastic had taken place in me, leaving me becalmed and conscious again of my blessings and proven values. By a Christian definition, I had sinned, coveting pleasures outwith my wedding vows and repairing – in a sensory *tour de force* – all too eagerly to the bed of my former lover. True, I had paid a price, so the ballast of recent memories intimated. My account was settled. But whatever vehicle had made my journey into the past or into the purlieus of mock reality possible – whether my keen perception of Ucello's fresco marshalling my consciousness into the backyard of Time (proof of which would no doubt propel psychic researchers into a state of mad scientific activity), or my baser instincts working as a hallucinogen – of one thing I was sure:

I had experienced an emotional renascence.

All the same, yes, my pen is ashamed to admit it, deep down and in the absence of supporting evidence, I did not a priori reject the possibility that I had returned to 'Time's First Dimension', Kant's philosophical concept of the past. For once, those crucial weeks were too cannily evocable, with every detail pencilled in my mind, to be dismissed with a shrug of the shoulders. Still too bold was their imprint – too recent, to all intents and purposes, their passage – for my memory to erase them on command, or to bury them in its hazy outbacks like some dangerous waste product. Yet increasingly – and what could reveal more convincingly the see-sawing state of my mind? – as the aircraft gobbled up the miles, and I picked at Alitalia's tin-foil Lasagne, I came to favour the view that a freak flare-up of my sexual drive, coupled with an unusually strong visual experience, had momentarily fogged up my sense of reality and time. Such a definition just made more sense and was easier to accept. Besides, it left plenty of room for rational arguments. And they now held that time-wanderings – the involvement of a human being in some metaphysical spoof – are fine fodder for the authors of sci-fi novels and time-tunnel scripts, fictive entertainment that carries the stamp of the purely imaginative. There, reality will always re-manifest itself with the last strip of celluloid or the final screen captions, and once a book has been put aside.

Tired of refereeing the mind's game of interpretations, I dozed off.

The captain's intercom, announcing our imminent arrival at Heathrow, ended my catnap. As the aircraft slowly descended through a thick sheet of clouds, leaving behind skies seemingly filled with eternal sunshine and feeding passengers with familiar views of urban sprawl, I felt as if I had just woken from an oppressive dream, the kind whose images are prone to linger, and which are difficult to separate from reality. Fastened to my seat, the cruising aircraft patiently awaiting landing instructions, I decided to pass the remaining minutes aloft by concentrating on things more tangible: I planned my days ahead.

I mentally drew up a job list, strictly according to priorities: Write copy for Lewis and drop into his office on way to town. Take Charles' blue suit to the cleaners. Ring plumber about the strange noise in the washing-machine motor. Remind Paul, when he is down for the weekend, to go and have his dental check-up. Start Christmas shopping early, to avoid seasonal rush. Organise January lecture. Ask Charles to stock up wine rack. Write Christmas cards . . .

I thought of the elegant blouse I had bought during a last-minute shopping spree. Made of silk, with a low neckline and wide, long sleeves, it came in a gorgeous glossy green, and I knew it flattered the colour of my hair and complexion. Charles would like its soft lines and, hopefully, its seductive cut. My suitcase also contained a few gifts: a second-hand copy of Seneca's philosophical essays in French for Charles, a designer T-short for Paul and an embroidered silk handkerchief for Val, who enjoyed luxurious accessories.

I was in no doubt: I was back at the wheel of my life, back in familiar waters. I resolved to give no more thought to what stood already at the periphery of consciousness, and which, for convenience's sake, if not for reasons of survival, I had neatly shelved as one of those queer moments of aberration or estrangement from reality, to which most of us, with varying intensity, fall prey at some time or other. Tomorrow beckoned solidly and demanding, but as pleasurably as the prospect of spring to northerners in the grip of winter.

19

As soon as I saw Charles, greying, bespectacled, yet still handsome, seigniorial in his stance even under what I had come to call the 'thinking arch' of his shoulders, I was conscious of a delicious commotion in my veins. Suddenly I was sixteen again, meeting my first date, the sixth-form heart-throb of the school, nicknamed James Dean II; I was the young Claire, being chatted up on the Ponte Vecchio by an attractive Florentine. And I could not help marvelling that after twenty years of marriage, returning from a short trip abroad, my heart should be thumping at the sight of my man.

'Hello, darling,' said Charles, as if I had been away on a day's shopping spree, or were back from a class. But I felt the tension behind the clichéd greeting, his inner reluctance to demonstrate feelings in public by embroidering words of welcome, something which like his most inner feelings his public-school Englishness preferred to express within his own hallowed domestic walls and, ideally, under soft lights and in the intimacy of a shared bed. Yet miracles happen even to comfortably-married couples, I suppose, for whom an ever-tightening emotional and intellectual bondage has replaced the magic, the tingling immediacy of their sexual relationship, an erosion purists and realists might style 'the confluence of mutually attracting and mesmerizing body chemistries having formed one serene flow over the years'.

As I loosened my cautious smile and eagerly met the spark in Charles' eyes, nothing could restrain the fireworks within us, and the way we kissed we might have been alone in the crowded Arrivals area.

Someone's luggage trolley finally shifted us, returned us to the hustle and bustle of the Terminal. For seconds we stood looking at each other as if struck by a sudden revelation.

'Glad you're back, darling,' said Charles, touching my shoulder in discreet support of his admission.

My reply, though equally succinct, radiated all the joy of my homecoming:

'I'm glad to be back, Charles.'

A bouquet of red roses graced the living-room which greeted me, warm and cosy, with the homely sight of Sunday newspapers, an empty whisky glass and Charles' green cashmere cardigan, the elbows of which cried out for patches or needles and darning wool. In the dining-room, the table was laid and a bottle of Bordeaux was breathing. In the kitchen, a shepherd's pie, prepared by my daily, was ready to go under the grill, and a pot of home-made lentil soup waited to be heated.

I soaked up the aura of peaceful, sophisticated domesticity, the harmony of shapes and colours, the taped euphonic sounds of Schumann's piano concerto. I greeted my favourite pictures, my pot plants, the mahogany table with the silver-framed photograph of Paul, and Charles' armchair which bore the imprint of a dream within a dream.

'How good it is to be home again,' I said, rejoicing in the knowledge that I had been wholly and uncompromisingly restored to my marriage, and stubbornly refusing to acknowledge that the impact my return was having on my senses was incompatible with an absence of a few days.

Charles did not read in bed that night, and I did not have to wait for the click of his spectacle case, nor the gritting winding-up sound of his alarm clock, before he made love to me as gently and virilely as the first time we slept together.

And in my response there was an element of gratitude and self-rediscovery, an intimation that the straying wife had found her way home.

Gradually, the sound of wind playing the bare trees outside the window like harps, and pummelling the loose hinges of a window, re-established themselves in my consciousness. So did the soft creamy light of the bedside lamps and, inert and symbolic of constancy, the familiar silhouettes of objects around the room.

In the road below, a car door banged shut, further afield a siren clamoured its way to the scene of a crime or an accident – sounds seemingly from another world, from outwith my loving domestic shell.

I was filled with a sense of completion. Yet in the vale of my happiness I realised that life would forthwith not revolve around similar feasts of love-making. More likely, Charles and I would continue to keep our love for each other on a steady keel, by cultivating the 'little things' in our marriage, which over the years had kept its light burning bright and steady. For inevitably, sooner or later, our renewed abandon was bound to bow to the laws of habit. Slave to routine, Charles would take up his bedtime ritual again, leaving me to seek sleep under the seal of his good-night kiss.

Strangely enough the prospect did not worry me. Not any more. For I knew that the depth of our feelings, whether celebrated by commemorative performances or not, would ensure a smooth ride into a phase of life when we would just want to grow old alongside each other, as if the best were still to come.

Paul came home for the weekend. Making his usual grande entrée, he dumped his bag and opened his arms wide.

'Hello, *mamma mia*,' he cried. 'Had a good trip? How's good old Florence?' And unzipping his jacket, 'I say, what's for lunch? I'm absolutely starving.'

His smile was infectious.

My motherly pride traced his handsome intelligent face, his athletic figure. Gracefully, I submitted to a rough hug and a peck on my cheek.

'Lovely to see you, son,' I said.

Our greetings over, I shot a critical look at Paul's washed-out jeans, which were split over the knees and frayed at the hems. With my generation's disapproval of slipshod attire I said:

'Son, you can't possibly walk around in those rags. Haven't you got a decent pair left?'

But Paul was off to the kitchen, inspecting the fridge and checking on preparations for lunch.

'We're having a ham-and-mushroom quiche with a salad,' I called after him, smiling.

Oh, yes, things were certainly back to normal.

Over the next few days I worked on my article, applying to it the cool detachment of a professional art columnist and critic, and dispassionately drawing from the wealth of my mental material and written notes. Everything seemed to fall into place, find its drift and strike an authentic note, without demanding an undue intellectual effort. But when in Lewis' absence I left my copy with one of his sub-editors, before meeting Val for lunch in town, I did so with a sigh of 'good riddance'.

Lewis rang me the following day.

'Congratulations, Claire, on an excellent piece of work. It's most evocative . . . hardly needs any editing. You know, it reads as if you really had been there at the time of the flood. Take alone your description of the damaged paintings and frescoes, and their subsequent restoration. The juxtapositions work very well, too. And I love your paragraph about Ucello's 'Deluge' and Cimabue's Cross. Then there are your background details. Some passages in fact suggest that you've had a very knowledgeable source, if not privileged access to documentation.'

'I did,' I said. 'Some old connections of mine. I made use of them!'

'Good girl!'

Once again I marvelled at the vividness of what I had come to accept as a state of mind outwith all rational modes of perception and, as such, defying analysis; of some sort of fantasy in which whatever I had read or heard in the past about the flood disaster in sixty-six, or which my mental archives had stored or deduced from photographs at the time, if not recently wishfully projected into a realm of credulity, had come to the fore, to line up images, make up new scenarios and warp my sense of time. The human mind is a curious thing, I told myself. Bertrand Russell called it 'a strange machine which can combine the materials offered to us in the most astonishing ways'. And my pen pauses, when I think of Matthew Arnold's estimation of the mind as 'the light with which the gods mock us'.

Had they mocked me?

20

Curiously enough it was Lewis who provided the final twist in the story.

'Claire,' he said, when he phoned me two days later, 'I've got hold of some archive pictures of the flood. Some of them have never been used and are quite startling. John's own shots are also on my desk. I think you ought to have a look at them. You could help me pick a few for the edition.'

'I'd *love* to see them,' I said, so as not to betray my lack of enthusiasm.

'Good. Could you possibly drop in today, preferably before noon? I realise it's rather short notice, but I'm afraid the layout people want them by tomorrow, and I won't be in this afternoon.'

The timing did not suit me at all. Lisa, the daily, had phoned to say she had caught 'a bug' and would not be in for a day or two. I had the washing-machine running, listening with apprehension to the rattling noise in the motor which I thought ought not to be there, and finding the mechanic's number engaged for the fifth time. On the stove a beef stew was simmering, and I had not even opened the mail yet. Besides, I had planned to structure my January lecture and go to the cleaners.

'I can make it in an hour,' I said. 'I'll combine town with some Christmas shopping.'

'Good idea, Claire. Early bird catches the best buys and all that, ha, ha!'

Sitting opposite Lewis, who was sporting a sedate suit and tie, I looked at the photographs he was passing me across the desk. I provided comments, answered questions and picked those I considered most suited to illustrate my article or enhance its slant.

Unruffled, safe in the rehabilitation of my emotions, I sieved photographic evidence: Florence under water or buried in mud; the heinous damage inflicted by water and oil, often indelibly, on the cultural treasures of the city, and where possible, restored in years of valiant, specialist labour.

'Now, look at this one,' said Lewis, loosening his tie, 'I thought I'd use this one for the edition. Could be one of our English students, one of the 'Angels of the Mud', as the Italians called them at the time, d'you remember? Colour is none too good, but it'll reproduce all right.'

He handed me a blown-up photograph.

My face fell. I squinted hard at the photograph, held it up towards the light to study it more closely. And now the blood surged away from my head on which each hair seemed to stand erect, and my heart pumped so loudly that I thought Lewis could hear it booming like a distant pile-driver. The picture danced in my hand, as my eyes were unable to refute the evidence:

I stared at a pretty young woman scraping mud from a heavily soiled tome. She wore mud-splattered rubber boots and yellow gloves, and a green apron over an outsize navy pullover. An encrusted strand of blond hair strayed from under her red-and-white dotted headscarf . . .

Suddenly I was shivering in the damp draught of a vault,

I was breathing the acrid air of mud, naphtha, mould and putrefaction. And out of such unpleasant, olfactorily repellent surroundings a voice reached me across the miles of memory: 'May I take a photograph of you, Miss?' This was when a gust of panic finally upset my composure and made me fall back in my chair, eyes half closed, my body seemingly bereft of any support.

'Claire, are you all right?' Lewis leaned across the desk and peered anxiously at me.

Ordering what was left of my self-control to match the emergency of the moment, I took a deep breath, sat up and replied:

'Yes, thank you, I'm fine. I suddenly felt faint. I think the rush this morning . . . and it is very warm in here.'

My laboured smile reassured the man behind his desk.

'That's because the damn radiators are blasting away,' he said. 'I must speak to the boiler-man or get maintenance to adjust them. Shall I open the window for you? Perhaps a glass of water or, better still, a cognac?'

'No, thank you, Lewis,' I replied, 'I feel better already. And I absolutely must be off.'

I got up, holding on to my smile like a shipwrecked person to a piece of flotsam. Half-way to the door, trying to play down the incident by setting solicitude against solicitude, I took refuge in the conventional: 'How is your boy? Back at school?'

Lewis beamed.

'Oh, he's fine, the rascal. Plaster will come off soon. By the way, Claire, I should like you to review the Italian Masters exhibition in January. I'll get in touch with you nearer the time. Thank you for coming in at such short notice.'

As was his custom, Lewis saw me to the door and shook my hand. The gesture had a strange soothing quality, I thought. Here was something that had not changed.

* * *

I did not take the narrow lift which always seems to convey someone or other, whether a copy writer, sub-editor, tea-lady or errand-boy. I needed time and space right then to face up to the new development. And walking down four flights of empty stairs without haste would make me come to a decision. It had to. For too much was at stake. I knew. Some knowledge, unless quietly accepted and left to age gracefully, will run riot in the mind. In the long run it will destroy one.

The sound of my heels hitting the stone treads echoed through the stairways like a metronome calling to mind the steady and remorseless forward thrust of Time. Clank, clank, clank . . . There must be no compromise, I thought, no delay, no wavering. Sometimes if a knot refuses to be untied, if must be cut. If a ghost won't lie down, it must be felled . . .

As I walked into the street I was mistress of the situation. I straightened up, squared my shoulders and looked ahead. The freedom of the afternoon beckoned. First, a coffee, then some Christmas shopping. A digital alarm clock and a new cardigan for Charles; for Paul a pair of jeans and a new squash racket. And I really must start my Christmas baking early this year. And I must not forget to buy a Ponsietta and some for fir branches for the living-room. And . . .

Firm steps carried me away.

I think I was smiling.

– fino –

Appendix

THE OLD CHRONICLES

extracts from the most celebrated chronicles
dealing with historic floods in Florence

THE CHRONICLES OF GIOVANNI VILLANI
(Book 7, Chapter XXXIV)

In the year 1269 on the night of the calends of October there was such great rain from heaven that, continuing for two nights and one day, all the rivers of Italy were swollen beyond anything ever seen before. The river Arno burst its bounds so immoderately that a great part of the city of Florence was flooded. Quantities of wood and timber borne by the river were piled up at the foot of the Ponte Santa Trinita so that the water behind spilled over into the city, where many people were drowned and many buildings destroyed . . .

On the fifth day of December (1288) there was a great rain in Florence and the surrounding countryside, so that the river Arno grew immoderately and overflowed its banks. This continued from morning to night, destroying palaces and buildings near the Pont Santa Trinita and doing much damage in the country about Florence . . .

In the year of our Lord 1333 on the calands of November, Florence being at that time more powerful and more prosperous than at any time in the century, it pleased God to send His judgement upon the city . . . The rain fell continuously for four days and four nights, increasing without restraint in so unusual manner that the very cataracts of heaven seemed to have opened . . . And thus many people were killed. And the Ponte Vecchio which was beaten by the wood and debris carried by the Arno was overcome by the fierce water, and the houses and shops which stood upon it were ruined, and at last all collapsed, and there remained but two of the piles in the centre . . . and (the water) left all the streets and the ground floor shops and houses and the cellars, which are so numerous in Florence, full of evil-smelling mud . . . And much merchandise was lost, and woollen cloth, and tools and furniture besides; and casks were broken, so that great quantities of wine went to waste . . . Certain it is that water sprang forth from the earth in many places, and even in the mountains, and therefore have we recounted of this flood the more fully, that it may be remembered; for no such adversity and damage came upon Florence since that time it was destroyed by Totila, the Scourge of God.

STORY OF HIS TIMES by GIOVANNI BATISTA ADRIANI
(Book 6)

At this time (1547) there came a very great flood which covered a large part of the city; At nine o'clock in the evening on 5th August a great rain began in Florence . . . it was so strong and persistent throughout the night that people said they had never seen anything like . . . The water came down in such a fury that it reached the walls of Florence before anyone suspected its approach . . . And (the water) advanced and flooded offices beneath the Palazzio Publico so swiftly that the clerks had no time to save the documents, many of which were lost. It then spread through other parts of the city and great damage was caused . . . It was in short the greatest flood that men had yet seen in this century . . . and the city was left filthy and much encumbered with mud and débris.

BALDINUCCI, OF THE LIFE OF BARTOLOMMEO AMMANNATI (1557)

On the twelfth day of September there came a ruinous rain which so increased the volume of the river that it began to overflow . . . destroying mills and other buildings, sweeping away bridges, and drowning many of the inhabitants in those parts . . .

SCIPIONE AMMIRATO TO DON VIRGINIO ORSINI, DUCA DI BRACCIANO (1559)

It rained continously through the last days of October . . . the river overflowed its banks in many places and poured through the lower parts of the city on both sides of the Arno . . . And the river also overflowed by way of the shops beneath the Corridore and over all the banks between the Ponte Vecchio and the Ponte dalla Carraia . . . a large beam beat against the side door of the Palazzo Ricosoli and broke it down . . . It seems that but by the Grace of God there were only two people killed in all the city – a goldsmith and a serving woman . . .

GUISEPPE AIAZZI, REPORT UPON THE FLOODING OF THE RIVER ARNO, 3 November 1844

... At first it rained intermittently, but later it continued without a break for many days and nights ... Early on Sunday, 3rd November, the Arno burst into Florence ... The water then began to spread through a large part of the city, first bursting the drains and sewers which debouch into the Arno, then flooding high over the river banks at many points ... All the inhabitants along the perimeter of the flood had their cellars and ground floors damaged by the foul water and mud; and many wells of pure and wholesome water were contaminated ... Meanwhile the flood continued to grow, and all but filled the arches of the Ponte Vecchio. The goldsmiths and jewellers who have their shops on the bridge ran in dismay to secure their most valuable items, then found that at any moment the timber and tree trunks carried on the flood might, as it were, cut the floor from beneath their feet and precipitate them into the inferno below ... The most needy of our people were justified in the faith they had in the charity of their fellow-citizens and of those foreigners who have made their homes among us, and who when called upon to aid those who had suffered in the fearful disaster, gave freely, *irrespective of rank and religion . . . It would be an unending task to list the quantities of foodstuffs that were lost, especially corn, wine and oil with the flooding of ground floors and cellars, both of merchants and private citizens. Casks and jars were dashed against walls and ceilings and smashed by the fury of the invading waters . . . In the large store rooms beneath the Uffici the chaos was indescribable, as the rarest manufactured goods and most precious foodstuffs were mishandled by the waters and reduced to ruin. Cases, casks and sacks were torn asunder, and sugar, coffee, spices and medicines, dye-stuff and other liquids were mixed together into a foul sea of mud, upon which floated articles of every description . . .*

DAWN, 4 NOVEMBER 1966

Florence slept as the waters rose . . .

Some reviews of *THE NAKED YEARS:*

"Evocatively written and gripping . . . compulsively readable."
Financial Times Educational Supplement

"Vivid, exciting, moving and compulsively readable."
Evening Times, Glasgow

"A most remarkable book."
Magnus Magnusson

"Seldom do I come across a book I know I'll remember for a long time to come. Thoroughly recommended."
The Sunday Post

"A remarkable human and social document."
The List

Some reviews of *THE ALIEN YEARS:*

"Constantly enjoyable, thanks to the author's marvellous gift for recall and the sensuous immediacy of her writing.'
D M Thomas

"A gripping sequel to the author's excellent wartime memoir. Highly readable."
The Sunday Post

TO ORDER FROM HILLCREST BOOKS

Marianne MacKinnon's books can be obtained or ordered from good bookshops throughout the United Kingdom – or direct from:

> Hillcrest Books, 54 Rosehill Road
> Torrance, Glasgow G64 4HF, Scotland

For signed copies and dedications, please order direct from Hillcrest Books.

Mail-order prices, inclusive of UK mainland post and packing, are:

> *The Deluge*, paperback, £5.99
> *The Naked Years*, paperback, £5.99
> *The Alien Years*, hardback, £9.99

For overseas orders, please include appropriate extra payment for postage.

Payment should be made to HILLCREST BOOKS by crossed UK cheque or postal order, or by Eurocheque or international money order drawn on sterling. Please do not send payments requiring currency conversion.

Orders will be posted immediately payments have cleared. Please be sure to write your name, address and post code in clear block capitals.